She loved him.

She would always love him, and whatever he felt for her, no matter how much more it was than simple physical passion, it was not love. It never could be. She was not Bianca.

His hands curled around her waist and his mouth pressed against the sensitive skin of her nape. "I love you, Danette."

She tore from his arms, stepping back and turning on him, her heart slamming in her chest. "Don't say that! You don't mean it!"

ROYAL BRIDES

The Scorsolini Princes:
proud rulers and passionate lovers
who need convenient wives!

*Welcome to this brand-new miniseries, set in glamorous
and exotic places known as the USIC (United Small
Independent Countries)—it's a world filled with
passion, romance and royals!*

Don't miss this new trilogy by Lucy Monroe:

THE PRINCE'S VIRGIN WIFE
July

HIS ROYAL LOVE-CHILD
August

THE SCORSOLINI MARRIAGE BARGAIN
September

HIS ROYAL LOVE-CHILD

BY
LUCY MONROE

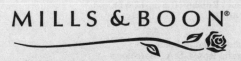

MILLS & BOON®

All the characters in this book have no existence outside the imagination of the author, and have no relation whatsoever to anyone bearing the same name or names. They are not even distantly inspired by any individual known or unknown to the author, and all the incidents are pure invention.

First published in Great Britain 2006
Harlequin Mills & Boon Limited,
Eton House, 18-24 Paradise Road, Richmond, Surrey TW9 1SR

© Lucy Monroe 2006

Standard ISBN 0 263 84833 7
Promotional ISBN 0 263 85122 2

Set in Times Roman 10½ on 12¼ pt.
01-0806-46527

Printed and bound in Spain
by Litografia Rosés, S.A., Barcelona

HIS ROYAL LOVE-CHILD

CHAPTER ONE

DANETTE MICHAELS closed the tabloid and put it down on the coffee table with careful precision.

Her hands were steady. It amazed her. A hurricane of pain was shaking her insides. She made no sound, though she wanted to scream. She wanted to rip the offending magazine to shreds, too. But she couldn't do either. If she so much as touched the tabloid again…if she gave vent to even a tiny bit of the storm tearing apart her soul, she was going to lose it completely.

She refused to do that. She'd spent years controlling her emotions, hiding both physical and mental pain while denying her tears. Ray's betrayal had made her cry and she'd sworn she wasn't going to let another man do that again. Not even Principe Marcello Scorsolini.

"He's just delish, isn't he?" Lizzy breathed, oblivious to the devastation her visit had wrought in Danette. She leaned forward and flipped the magazine open again, and pointed to the picture that was the source of Danette's current mental agony. "Can you imagine being that woman?"

Danette looked down at the picture. She didn't want to. It hurt, but she couldn't help herself. Her eyes were drawn by an emotion as powerful as the love that lay bleeding at the bottom of her heart. The *need to know*, and a desperate hope that her vision had deceived her the first time.

It had not.

The picture was exactly what she thought it was. It showed the drop-dead gorgeous president of the Italian arm of Scorsolini Shipping dancing with an equally attractive woman at his father's birthday bash on Scorsolini Island. They were practically molded to one another's bodies. Prince Marcello was smiling and the woman looked like a beautiful, sleek cat who had just copped a whole bowl of the richest cream.

How could Danette have been so stupid that she'd allowed herself to get involved with *this* man…to actually believe that they had enough in common where it counted?

She'd fallen into his arms with about as much self-preservation as a lemming following the pack leader off the side of a cliff. She'd given him her virginity and asked for nothing in return but his overwhelming passion. He'd offered her his fidelity, but that picture made her doubt the sincerity of the gift.

Contrary to what he had told her, her prince was the king of the playboys. Was she terminally stupid where men were concerned, or simply unlucky?

"Earth to Danette. Hello, is anyone in there?" Lizzy's voice penetrated Danette's crushing thoughts.

"What?"

"Where were you at, *chica*? Don't tell me you were thinking about work."

"Something like that," Danette said in a strained voice. In her mind, her job and her lover were inexorably linked.

"I *said,* can you imagine being her?"

Only too well, except when Marcello held Danette close like that, she was never wearing a designer original ball gown. Most of the time, she wasn't wearing anything at all. "Yes."

Lizzy laughed. "You've got a better imagination than me then."

"Not really."

"Are you okay?" Lizzy asked, her face creased with concern. "You seem out of it, and more than just your normal preoccupation with being the original Wonder Woman at work."

Danette forced herself to look away from the picture and at her small, blond friend. They were both Americans, but that was where the similarity ended. Lizzy was five feet even with the body of a pocket Venus and short blond hair that fell in wild ringlets around her heart-shaped face. She also had an infectious smile that had drawn Danette to her immediately.

Danette, on the other hand, had slight curves, a very slender build, a neck that Marcello said looked like a graceful swan's, but which she felt was too long, average looks he called refreshingly natural, and average height that felt very tiny beside his six-foot-two-inch frame. Her chin-length mouse-brown hair was straight and even when she tried to curl it, it never held. So she'd given up trying.

Marcello said it felt like silk against his fingertips and he loved the fact she didn't starch it with lots of product, but the blonde he was holding so closely in the picture certainly looked made up to the nines. So much for Marcello's evinced preference for the *unadorned lily*. It was obvious he liked hothouse orchids just fine.

That picture made her wonder if she hadn't fooled herself about Marcello just as badly as she had with Ray.

She tried for a smile, but failed. She settled for a sigh. "I'm fine. Just tired. I've been working hard on the Cordoba project."

"With the hours you put in, it's no wonder you don't have a social life."

But Danette did have a social life…a secret one that gave her more pleasure than she'd ever dreamed was possible. At least it had until this moment.

She managed to force the smile this time, though she wasn't sure it was a very convincing one. "You know how it is."

Lizzy's smile was genuine, if tinged with worry. "What I know is that you work too hard."

"Not really. I love my job."

"I love my job, too, *chica*, but you don't see me spending every waking moment dedicated to it." Lizzy winked. "I've got better things to do with my off hours. Speaking of, I've got to get going…you sure you don't want to come down to the taverna with the rest of us?"

Danette shook her head. "Sorry, but I think I'll go for an early night."

Lizzy sighed and shook her head, her blond curls bouncing. "You need to get out more."

"I do get out." With Marcello, and nowhere anyone from Scorsolini Shipping was likely to run into her.

Lizzy just snorted, then her expression turned calculating. "If you aren't there, Ramon from sales is going to be disappointed."

"I doubt it."

"The guy has the hots for you, he's good-looking,

great at his job, and he's single. Why not come down, spend some time with him? See where it goes."

"Ramon has had four different girlfriends in the last six months…he's a bad risk." But she had to swallow a burble of hysterical laughter as she realized what she'd just said.

No worse risk existed in the relationship stakes than Marcello Scorsolini.

"All of life is a gamble, or haven't you learned that yet?" Lizzy asked as she got up to go.

"Some chances are more worth taking than others."

"And you don't think Ramon is one of them?"

Danette sighed. "I don't know, but not tonight. I'm sure about that much, all right?"

"Okay." Lizzy smiled again and reached out to hug her. "Get some sleep. I'll see you at work tomorrow."

Danette hugged her back. As she stepped away, she remembered all the times she'd encouraged her friend, Tara, to go for it with Angelo Gordon, but this was different. No one could compete with Marcello…not even the sexy, charming Ramon from sales. "Have fun tonight."

"We will." Lizzy turned to leave.

"You forgot your magazine."

"Keep it," Lizzy tossed over her shoulder on her way out the door. "It'll give you something to read before bed."

The door shut behind the other woman before Danette could respond.

She didn't want to read the tabloid. She didn't want to look at it. She didn't want it in her apartment, but when she picked it up to throw away, she found herself rereading every single word of the article about King Vincente's birthday party. It was a four-page spread with tons of pictures, a few quotes and enough innuendo to sink an oil tanker.

She was staring at the picture of Tomasso and the woman dancing when a peremptory knock sounded on her door.

She lived in what had once been the groundskeeper's cottage on a large estate on the outskirts of Palermo. The family still occupied the main house and the security system was top-notch. Angelo and Tara had helped her find the place and she was really grateful. Even though Angelo had arranged for her job, she'd wanted to make it on her own in Italy from that point forward. So, she had refused her parents' offer to help her buy another condo like the one she'd had in Portland, or in procuring what they considered an acceptable place of habitat for their one and only child.

The groundskeeper's cottage with security services provided by the main house had been a compromise they could live with.

Because her home was far from the main road and the security was so good, she didn't worry about getting unwanted guests. However, Marcello had drilled into her enough times never to open the door without checking first to be sure she knew her visitor, that she automatically did so now.

It was him.

She didn't know why that should shock her, but it did. After seeing the article, her mind had told her he no longer belonged to her…if he ever had. Therefore, why would he bother showing up on her doorstep?

Yet, there he stood on the other side of her door looking like the epitome of Sicilian male perfection. From his golden-brown hair styled casually to enhance his sculpted features, to the tips of his Gucci leather shoes, he exuded delectable masculine appeal. He also looked tired, the skin around his cobalt-blue eyes lined with fatigue.

He'd probably been too busy partying to sleep. Even as the unpleasant thought surfaced, she was forced to dismiss it. She knew better.

He'd been gone on a business trip for more than a week before his father's birthday party. They'd spoken on the phone every night and he'd made it clear he was pushing himself and everyone around him to finish.

Only seeing the picture had made her think that he wouldn't come straight to her from the airport. Why would he when he had beautiful, sophisticated women like the one in the photo to spend his time with?

Perhaps it was an irrational line of reasoning, but she wasn't at her logical best at the moment. He knocked a second time, the staccato rap and his scowl communicating his impatience at being kept on the doorstep.

She opened the door and then stood staring mutely at his large frame as it filled her doorway.

His sensual lips transformed from a frown to an enticing smile. "Good evening, *tesoro mio*. Are you going to let me in?"

"What are you doing here?"

His eyes narrowed, the smile disappearing as quickly as it had come. "What kind of question is that? I have not seen you for more than a week. My plane landed not an hour ago...where else would I be?"

Six months ago, when they'd begun their affair, the question would have been ludicrous. He had made it a point of seeing her only a couple of nights a week, but as the weeks progressed the number of nights they spent together increased until they were practically living together...albeit in secret.

"Maybe spending time with your new girlfriend?"

He stepped into the small cottage, forcing her to move backward if she didn't want him touching her. And she didn't. Not right now. Maybe never again.

She tripped backward with speed, not stopping until she was several feet away.

"What other girlfriend?" he asked, enunciating each word with quiet precision as he pushed the door shut behind him and then followed her across the room.

She lifted the gossip rag toward him. "This one."

He stared down at the magazine and then took it from her hand to look more closely. His eyes skimmed the pages, his expression turning to one of disdain before he tossed it to the coffee table behind her. "That is nothing more than a scandal sheet. Why were you reading it?"

"Lizzy brought it over. She thought it was a hoot to read an article about the big boss. What difference does it make how it came into my possession? Dismissing it as a low form of journalism isn't going to make the pictures go away or the behavior that got caught in the camera lens for that matter."

"Nothing untoward was caught on film."

"You don't think so?"

"I danced with a few women at my father's birthday party, smiled at some, talked. There is no crime in that."

"Not if you weren't attached, no."

His frown intensified, eyes that usually looked on her with indulgent affection going wintry. "You know I will not tolerate a possessive scene, Danette."

She almost laughed. He sounded so darn arrogant it wasn't hard to believe he was a prince, only that he was the youngest son. That kind of egotism should be reserved for the heir to the throne.

"Fine. Leave and we won't have one."

He jolted as if she'd slapped him. "You want me to leave? I've just arrived."

"Well, since apparently the only thing you want me for is sex and I'm definitely not in the mood after seeing those pictures, you might as well."

"I have never said that." He cursed volubly in Italian. "Where did that come from? Why would you say such a thing? I do not see you as a body without a brain."

"Good, because I have one, and it's telling me that if I was more than a body in your bed, I would have been by your side at your father's party, not reading about it in a gossip rag two days later and having to see pictures of you flirting with other women."

"You know why you were not at my side."

"Because you don't want anyone to know about me! You're ashamed of me, aren't you?" she asked, slipping one more notch into pain-induced irrationality and unable to do a thing to prevent it. Which terrified her more than the pain itself. She had always been able to control her emotions, no matter how devastating, but what she felt for him was too big.

Apparently he thought she'd gone over the edge, too, because he stared at her as if she'd lost her mind. "You are insane tonight. First you accuse me of having another woman, then you say I see you as nothing but a sex toy…or as good as." He shook his head as if to clear it. "This is crazy. *I am not ashamed of you.*"

"But you don't want anyone to know about me."

"For your own sake." He swore again and tunneled his long brown fingers through his hair. "You know how invasive the paparazzi can be. The minute they got wind of my relationship with you, you would be watched your every waking moment. You would not be able to go to a public restroom without having a reporter ready to take your picture from under the stall next to your own."

"It wouldn't be that bad. I'm not big news."

"But I am. I have lived my whole life the son of one of the relatively few royal couples in history to have divorced. I had no privacy in my marriage. Bianca had to travel everywhere with bodyguards not only for her personal security, but to protect her from the intrusive press. I have told you this."

Danette said nothing. The logical part of her brain knew he spoke the truth, but she could not make herself admit it. Even if her mind told her that he was determined to keep their relationship private because he valued it so much, her heart said that a relationship that had to be hidden wasn't valuable enough.

The way he'd been dancing with the blonde certainly made it look like he valued *her*.

He sighed. "I developed a playboy facade after Bianca's death to protect myself and the woman I truly wanted to be with. You know this. We have discussed it before."

She did know it. She had even seen it as something deeply personal they had in common. After all, hadn't she developed an outgoing, flirtatious image to hide the very private person she was beneath the facade? She'd seen his playboy reputation the same way once he explained it to her. Only that photo implied the persona was the man.

It made a mockery of the love she'd discovered she felt for him. Love wasn't supposed to be like this. It wasn't supposed to hurt so much. It was supposed to make life beautiful, to empower the lover...but all she ever got from it was pain and a horrible sense of insecurity.

"How many women have you *truly wanted to be with* since Bianca?" she demanded, feeling waspish and hurt and unable to hold back the ugly question.

"That is none of your business."

"Apparently most of your life is none of my business."

"That is not true."

"You don't share it with me."

"That is a lie." He looked like he wanted to shake her. "You get more of my time than anyone else. Did I not work twenty-hour days while I was gone so that I could fly back to you after the birthday party rather than returning to our shipping office in Hong Kong?"

He rubbed his eyes, his face drawn with exhaustion and reflecting disappointment. "We spend practically every evening together doing more than sharing our bodies and you know this, *tesoro mio*. We have been to the theater, out to dinner many times…we have put puzzles together because it is something you enjoy doing and you have taught me to play odd American card games. The only part of myself I do not share with you is the public spotlight. I understood that was not something you craved. Was I wrong? Do you wish to be known as the latest lover for a Scorsolini prince?"

His sarcasm didn't even faze her. "If it means I don't have to see pictures of you plastered against another woman, yes."

He shook his head. "We were dancing. That is all. It meant nothing. You must know this."

"All I know is that you two looked like you were getting ready to make a hasty exit from the party and find someplace private to continue dancing."

"You are jealous." He shook his head. "There is no need."

"I'm hurt!"

"Only because you do not trust me."

"How can I?"

"I told you that for as long as we are together, our relationship would be exclusive. I gave you my word. You have known me for a year, intimately for half as long. When have you ever known me to break it?"

"I don't like being your dirty little secret."

"What we share is not dirty, and you are a secret because our relationship is so special to me that I do not want to lose it," he gritted out between clenched teeth.

She averted her face, refusing to answer, and the silence stretched between them. She sensed his movement, but was still shocked when one of his hands brushed the hair back from her temple and then slipped down to cup her chin. He gently turned her face until their gazes met.

"I am very sorry if the pictures hurt you."

She knew he considered this a major climb-down, and to give him credit, for him it *was*. He had started the conversation off with a refusal to have a scene and was now apologizing. He was too darn perfect to have to apologize much and too powerful to be forced into giving one even when he was wrong in most cases, but it didn't make her feel any better.

What difference did an apology make when it wasn't accompanied by the assurance the offense would not happen again?

Seeing the picture had hurt her. A lot. She felt like her heart was being ripped into shreds even now.

"Just tell me one thing," she said. "How would you feel if our positions were reversed? What if you were the one looking on at me flirting with other men?"

His jaw clenched as if the thought was not a pleasant one, but then he visibly relaxed his tense facial muscles. "In order to keep our relationship private, I must act naturally at public social functions. It would be entirely *unnatural* for me to ignore a roomful of women. Speculation would be rife if I was to do so and the paparazzi would soon begin looking for my secret liaison or making assumptions about my masculine urges, or worse."

"That's not an answer to my question."

He was a master at redirection, which made him a force to reckon with in the business world and not much more user-friendly in a relationship. But she'd been with him six months and worked for him six months before that. She knew most of his techniques by now and wasn't about to be swayed by them.

"It is all the answer you need. This is not about tit for tat. My behavior was necessary."

"And if I behaved similarly *out of necessity* it would not bother you?"

"The occasion does not arise."

"Are you sure about that?" She paused, giving him a moment to let the question prick at his arrogant certainty. "Just because I'm not gossip-column worthy doesn't mean I never flirt with other men."

"And do you?" he asked with an indulgence that said more clearly than anything else could how little he worried about the possibility.

"I haven't, because I considered myself taken, but I realize now that I shouldn't have."

CHAPTER TWO

"YOU *are* taken," Marcello said forcefully, no indulgence in evidence any longer.

"Not if you aren't, I'm not."

He let out a breath of obvious frustration. "It is not a matter of not considering myself in a relationship…it is merely that were I to ignore the overtures of other women completely, it would lead to too much speculation."

"Whereas my loyalty does not?"

"It is not a matter of loyalty," he denied, anger starting to curl around the edges of his forced patience.

"Yes, it is."

"I told you, it is a matter of expediency."

"And if me turning down invitations led to the same speculation that worries you, would that be reason for me to respond similarly? To go out with other men, to flirt with them?"

"I did not go out with anyone! I danced…I talked…I flirted as Italian men do, but I did not touch anyone as I touch you. *I did not want to*."

"You had that woman's body as close to yours as you could get with your clothes on."

"It did nothing for me."

"Is that supposed to matter?"

"It should."

"Why?"

"It tells you that despite your insecurities, you are special to me."

"So special I'm a big, dark secret no one in your life knows about."

"So special that only the thought of seeing you turns me on. Holding another woman with her body pressed to mine does not because she is not you."

She didn't want to be moved by his description, but her susceptible heart told her that *was* unique…particularly for a man like Marcello Scorsolini.

He put his hands on her shoulders, his thumbs brushing her collarbone in a way he knew made her shiver. "The only woman I want, the only woman I crave to touch and be touched by right now, is you."

If he hadn't tacked the *right now* on, his statement would have been perfect.

He crowded close to her until their bodies brushed. "You are the only woman I *want* to hold this close. Everything at the party was window dressing…it meant nothing. Believe me, *tesoro*. Please."

The *please* did it. This man was not accustomed to begging. For anything. She had to be special to him, or he would have walked out when she started being difficult. Because he could have any woman he wanted…of that she was certain. And he made it clear he wanted only her.

"You didn't have sex with the beautiful blonde?"

He crushed her to him, his arms winding around her in a possessive hold that shook her. "No, *porca miseria*! I would never do that to you, *mio precioso*. I promise you."

She believed him and the relief she felt was incredible. "Good, because I would never stay with a player."

He laughed, the sound strained. "I am no player. I am not even the playboy the press paints me. I thought you knew this. I thought you knew *me*."

"I did. I do, but a picture is worth a thousand words."

"Only if you are speaking the same language as the photographer. What that journalist caught on film was two strangers dancing, nothing more. But look at the picture we paint, *amante*. Look and see the difference between eyes hot to possess and a social smile that meant nothing. Look at my hands which tremble with the need to touch you, but which held the other woman with total indifference."

His words did indeed paint a picture more powerful than the one in the scandal sheet. And the feel of his body pressed against hers backed it up. He needed her and she needed him. She'd missed him so much.

"If you are not a playboy, then what are you?" she asked provocatively.

"A mere man who wants you very much."

She could feel how much he wanted her and it made her insides melt.

Her mind started short-circuiting as it always did when he touched her, but she could still think straight enough to say, "Maybe we need to go public with our relationship. I don't like seeing pictures like that, Marcello. They hurt."

He kissed the corner of her mouth, the bridge of her nose, her forehead and then her lips with aching tenderness. "You are too sweet, *cara*. The press would pulverize you and I could not bear to watch, but I will do all that I can to make sure you are not hurt this way again."

That was something, she supposed, but she wanted to argue that she could handle the press. She was strong. She'd had to be her whole life. But her mouth was too busy kissing his to utter the words that needed saying.

The next morning, Marcello was gone when she woke up and so was the scandal rag, she noticed.

However, there was a red rose on his pillow and a note beside it. It read:

Cara,
Thank you for last night. I treasure our times together and the generosity of your affection for me.
M

He'd never left her a note before. His paranoia about privacy extended to not leaving any evidence of their relationship for others to find. This was a huge departure for him. It had to be significant. Maybe he was thinking about her desire to go public…maybe he was beginning to see that she was right.

The one thing she knew for certain was that his desire for her was not feigned. If he'd found relief with a convenient body while he was away from her, she was a monkey's uncle.

He'd been way too hungry. They'd made love into the early hours of morning and he had told her repeatedly how much he missed her, how beautiful she was to him, how special. All the words her vulnerable heart longed for.

Except the three that really mattered, but then she'd never said them to him, either.

She'd always worried they would spell the end to their relationship. She'd assumed he would reject that sort of emotional tie. He'd been so clear at the beginning of their affair that it could only ever be just that. An affair with a beginning and an end and no happily ever after. She'd wanted him so much and had been so impressed with his honesty after Ray's lies that she'd said yes.

And until she'd seen that picture in the tabloid, she'd never once regretted her choice. Marcello was an incredible lover and the time they spent together out of bed was equally fulfilling. He'd made their first time together very special and every time after.

His desire to keep their relationship underwraps had suited her down to the ground at first. She was too private a person to want to share their intimacy with the world at large. In that, too, she and Marcello were really alike. She'd seen what the gutter press could do with her friend Tara. At first, Danette had been only too happy to avoid the possibility of experiencing anything ugly and intrusive like that herself.

But beyond that, she had feared that if word of her relationship with Marcello got out, she would have to deal with interference from her well-meaning but over-protective parents. She'd also been concerned that her job might be affected, no matter how much Marcello did not want that to happen. She wanted to earn her advancement and did not want others speculating what her time between the sheets with the president of the company meant for her career.

She'd spent her whole life up to now under the watchful and overly intrusive eye of her family. It was important to her to prove that the strength it had taken to beat the scoliosis that had threatened her ability to walk, and even her life, spilled over into the rest of her existence as well.

Which was one of the reasons she hadn't wanted love or a long-term commitment in the beginning, either. She'd spent years in a sort of self-imposed isolation because of the brace she'd worn until she was nineteen to correct the deforming curve in her spine. And she'd wanted to feel what it was to be a woman. She'd wanted to date, to kiss, to heavy pet and ultimately to make love.

She'd wanted Marcello beyond reason and independently of finer feelings…or at least that was what she'd thought.

When she'd arrived in Italy, the farthest thing from her mind had been a desire to get into another relationship. She'd been bent on proving she wasn't as stupid as Ray's betrayal had made her feel. The first time they met, Marcello had unwittingly given her the means to do so.

She'd been feeling frustrated with herself because Angelo had arranged for her job, wondering if she could ever make it entirely on her own. She didn't know if everyone was so nice because they liked her, or because they wanted to do Angelo a favor…or at least please their boss who had extended the favor to his good friend.

She'd been in the middle of a royal bout of insecurity when Marcello made his first appearance at her desk. "You are the friend of Angelo Gordon's wife, are you not?" he'd asked without bothering to introduce himself.

She'd known who he was of course and even how he preferred to be addressed within Scorsolini Shipping. "Yes, Signor Scorsolini. I'm Danette Michaels."

"Angelo speaks highly of you."

"I'm glad. I loved my job with his company."

"But you wanted a change of venue, to see some of the world?" he asked with a blue gaze that could probe into the very depths of her soul.

"Yes."

He nodded. "You realize that my good friend's reputation in my eyes depends a great deal on your performance here." He didn't say it unkindly, or as if in warning, more like he was confirming something she already knew.

But it was news to her…welcome news. It gave her a target to aim for and said that, far from awarding her special treatment, he would expect more from her than his other employees. The words were like honey to her ears and she lapped them up. "I won't let either of you down."

"I do not doubt this. I am sure that because you came to work for me on his recommendation, you will work twice as hard to prove that he was smart to recommend you."

"You're right, I will." And it was a vow.

He smiled then, giving her her first taste of mind numbing physical awareness. "Don't work *too* hard. But I do not believe you will let either of us down."

And in proving him right, she made the job *her* personal triumph. Every success she achieved was a gift she consciously gave to both men who had chosen to believe in her and subconsciously gave to herself. When she had been promoted and given her own office after only four months because of her diligence, Marcello had called to personally congratulate her and Angelo had sent her an e-mail thanking her for making him look so good to his friend.

It had all been very feel good and laid a strong foundation for her growing confidence as an independent woman. Marcello asking her out had added to that confidence though she'd definitely been leery of him to begin with.

Danette worked on her sales projection report, determined to make her boss glad he'd promoted her and given her a private office. If there was a part of her that wanted to impress the president of the company, too, well, that was to be expected.

After all, he'd arranged for her to get her current job on the recommendation of his friend and she didn't want him to regret that choice, either. It had nothing to do with the fact that every time she saw him, her breathing and pulse rate went wacko.

She wasn't interested in risking her heart again and for sure not with a man of Prince Marcello Scorsolini's playboy reputation.

"Do you realize the time, Danette?"

Her head snapped up at the sound of the company president's voice coming from her open doorway.

"Signor Scorsolini!" She jumped up from her chair, looking around her, trying to focus on the now while her mind was still stuck on sales figures.

The hall outside her office was on dimmed lighting for after hours and the silence surrounding them told her that she was one of the few people left in the building. The small clock on her desk said it was eight o'clock.

Her mouth rounded in an, "Oh…" and then she gave him a rueful grimace. "No wonder my legs feel like they've petrified in one position."

"You work too hard."

She laughed as she stretched, realizing as she did so that her entire body was seriously cramped from sitting at her desk for so long. "That's a bit like the pot calling the kettle black, don't you think? Your workaholic hours are legendary around here."

"I do not expect my employees to give up all life outside of work in order to serve Scorsolini Shipping." He watched her stretch with disturbing intensity. "It is not the same for me. I have more reasons than most company presidents to make sure my business is a success."

"What do you mean?" she asked curiously as she smoothed her hair with a nervous hand.

The flirtatious facade she had created to deal with men deserted her in his company. She was lucky to string two syllables together that made sense when he spoke to her.

"The people of my country rely on the income from Scorsolini Shipping worldwide to maintain a standard of living in line with the other industrialized nations."

"You mean Isole dei Re?"

"Yes, naturally."

She didn't want to sit down again, but she felt exposed standing there behind her desk. She compromised by busying herself stacking the papers related to the sales projection report. It was the way he was looking at her...not at all like a boss looks at his employee.

More like a predator sizing up its prey.

She searched her mind for something to say. "I don't understand how Isole dei Re can be so reliant on this division of Scorsolini Shipping. There are only a handful of your countrymen and women employed here."

"You know this how?"

"I asked."

"It is interesting that you care." His still predatory gaze probed her speculatively.

"Everything about the company I work for interests me."

Marcello moved further into the room. "And the man you work for, does he interest you, I wonder?"

"You didn't just say that." She stared at him, shock coursing through her.

He smiled, his blue eyes full of knowing amusement. "I did, but we will leave it for the moment and I will answer your other question. While I do not employ many of my country's subjects, half of the net profits of all Scorsolini companies are paid into the national treasury and used to maintain and improve the country's infrastructure."

"You mean things like hospitals?" she asked fascinated. It had never occurred to her that the royal family gave back to their country on such an overwhelming scale.

"That and roads, schools, police and fire departments…the many things citizens of larger countries take for granted as being paid for by tax dollars."

"Wow."

"The money must come from somewhere."

"And Scorsolini Shipping is it?"

"Along with what tax dollars we do receive in revenue and the other enterprises of our country. My older brother, Tomasso, has recently supervised the discovery of lithium mines on Rubino. He has taken Scorsolini Mining and Jewels to an unprecedented level." His voice rang with pride in his brother's achievement.

"Funny, that's what Angelo Gordon told me you had done with the Italian arm of Scorsolini Shipping."

"My father and older brother are pleased with my efforts."

"They should be." And then she blushed at the vehemence of her words.

But he smiled, apparently pleased by her words. "My older brother, Claudio, has recently informed me that when he ascends to the throne, he and Tomasso have agreed that I will take over the entire shipping company while Tomasso maintains his position as head of Scorsolini Mining and Jewels."

"Did that surprise you?"

He nodded, coming closer, his presence filling her senses. "Normally the second son would take that position and I would either continue as I am or take Tomasso's position, but because he has taken that side of our family's holdings so far and my brothers and father are content with my performance here, I will be given the honor."

"That's wonderful! I suppose you celebrated by working a few extra twenty-hour days," she teased, knowing from the company grapevine that was exactly what he'd been doing lately.

He came around the desk and leaned against it, not six inches from where she stood. "Just as you have done?"

"Touché." She stopped in the act of reaching for the papers she'd stacked so she could file them. Doing so would require leaning into him and her senses were headed toward overload as it was. "I just don't want my boss to regret his decision to promote me," she said a trifle breathlessly.

"I also feel this need…in relation to the confidence my family has put in me."

His scent was teasing at her olfactory senses and she wanted to get closer, which was insane under the circumstances. "I guess…um…that we have something in common."

He reached out and touched her. Just a light brush against her cheek, but she felt paralyzed by it.

"Perhaps more than this single thing," he suggested.

Her face tingled where he had brushed it. "I can't imagine that we could have much else. Our lives are very different."

"Perhaps, but I think you are wrong. Will you have dinner with me tonight to find out?"

"What?" She shook her head, trying to clear it. The president of Scorsolini Shipping had asked her out on a date?

"I would like you to have dinner with me."

"But…"

"I like you, Danette, and I hope you like me, too." But his confident smile said he already knew she did, that he knew exactly the effect his nearness was having on her body.

"Of course I like you, but you asked me out on a date. I'm not your type."

"And you base this assumption on what?"

"Everybody knows you date really gorgeous women."

"You are beautiful."

She snorted at that. "I have a mirror. I'm nothing like the women you normally have your picture taken with."

"That is window dressing…a facade I present to the world to keep my private life private." He looked so sincere, but he couldn't be serious.

"But—"

"Come to dinner with me and see what kind of man I am when the paparazzi are not present with their insidious cameras."

"My job…" she said uncertainly.

"I make you this promise, Danette. Your job will not be influenced for good or for ill regardless of what happens or does not happen between us."

"So, if I say no to your dinner invitation?" she asked.

"I will be disappointed, but that will have no impact on your employment, advancement or type of opportunities given here at Scorsolini Shipping. To be fair, I must also tell you that even if you were to become my lover, that would not impact those same things in a positive way, either."

"I never for a moment would have expected them to."

"You are very naive."

"There's nothing naive about believing that a person should earn their job advancement."

He smiled, but his eyes were serious. "I like that about you and I agree."

"Good."

"So, will you allow me to take you to dinner?"

Every logical impulse in her body screamed at her to tell him no. She didn't want to get into a relationship, but dinner wasn't exactly a promise for the future. Maybe he was only interested in friendship. But he'd mentioned being her lover. That implied a lot more than chatting over coffee.

Oddly enough, it was the prospect of the *more* that had her so horribly tempted. She'd dated so little in her life and she'd never spent so much as half an hour with a man as intriguing as Marcello. Not unless you counted

Angelo Gordon, but he belonged to her friend and even he didn't stir her latent sexuality the way that Marcello did.

Ray certainly never had, the lying sneak.

This wasn't about love and happily ever after, she told herself, it was about experiencing feelings she'd denied herself far too long.

"Okay. I'll have dinner with you."

CHAPTER THREE

HE TOOK her to a small, family run restaurant outside of Palermo. It was a quarter to nine by the time they reached it. She'd learned Europeans often ate late. The owner was more than happy to give them a table.

As a dinner companion, Marcello lived up to every concept she had of him. He was charming, attentive and so sexy that her body thrummed with an awareness she'd never experienced with another man.

He poured her a second glass of the rich red wine he'd ordered with dinner. "So, Angelo said you were ready for a change and that is why you came to Sicily."

She'd noticed since coming to Palermo that Sicilians made a distinction between themselves and other Italians, as if they were their own separate country. Marcello did the same thing even though technically, he was from another country altogether. She had heard that his mother was Sicilian. Perhaps that accounted for it.

"Yes, I needed a change."

"Was there a man involved?"

Strangely she did not find his question intrusive. In an inexplicable way, she felt she could tell him almost anything. "Yes."

"What happened?" he asked with an expression that compelled her to share her deepest secrets with him.

"How do you do that?"

"What?"

"Make me feel like I should tell you everything in my head."

"Ah…there is a lot more to being the head of an international business than being able to count money."

She laughed. "I know that, but I wasn't aware that playing the role of father confessor was part of it."

"You would be surprised. Now tell me about the boyfriend."

"I thought he loved me, but he used me to get pictures of Tara and Angelo so he could break into tabloid journalism."

"He was the one responsible for those stories about them in the scandal rags last year?"

"Yes. They hurt Tara, a lot. She'd been savaged by the press once before and Ray's antics got her fired before Angelo found out what had happened."

"I hate the tabloids."

"But you're in them so often."

"Like I told you, I create a facade for them to latch on to so they leave my real life alone."

She'd done the very same thing as a small child. She'd created an image of an outgoing, confident girl that hid her private thoughts and feelings. No matter how intrusively doctors, or even her own parents, played their roles in her life, there was an interior Danette who remained sacrosanct to her alone.

Knowing they shared such a coping mechanism made her feel close to him in a way she would not have thought possible.

"Tell me more about Ray," Marcello said.

"There isn't much to tell. He was looking for the main chance and took it, not caring who he hurt or how much he hurt them. I think that's what devastated me the most. He couldn't have known my best friend was going to get involved with a media interest like Angelo Gordon, or that her notoriety would be so easily revived."

At least that's what she'd thought. "Our relationship started out for the usual reasons...I think. My family is wealthy and maybe he figured all along that I might take him into circles he could use to advance his career goals, but I really think that he saw the main chance and just went for it."

"And this hurt you?"

"Very much, but I'm over him now." And she was. It had happened faster than she'd thought it could.

The move to Italy had been the right choice.

"The betrayal by a lover is the most devastating."

"He wasn't my lover, thank goodness."

"So, the relationship wasn't very old?"

"That depends on how you define old. We were together for a few months."

"And he did not take you to bed?"

"It wasn't for lack of trying on his part," she said, stung that Marcello should think that she wasn't fanciable.

"No doubt. Why did you hold back from him?"

"It never felt right. It made him angry, but I didn't realize how much. He said some very cutting things when we broke up."

"I see."

"Do you? What do you see, Signor Scorsolini?"

"First that you must call me Marcello when we are away from the company."

She smiled despite the heavy feelings in her heart from her trip down memory lane. "All right."

"Second, that the man was a fool and obviously not very good in the seduction stakes."

"Or I'm not easily seduced."

"Be assured, I love a challenge."

She gasped at his blatant claim and the implication of it. "I'm not looking for that right now."

"But you have found it, as I will delight in showing you. I want you and I intend to have you."

But he didn't push for even a good-night kiss when he took her home that night. And it was the same on the three dates they had after that over the next two weeks. No matter what he had said, he seemed perfectly happy with a platonic friendship, while her physical awareness of him grew with every moment spent in his company.

She even started having sexy dreams about him. She would wake up feeling embarrassed by her obvious desire and disturbed by the strength of it...not to mention how easily he'd infiltrated her subconscious as well as her conscious life.

He'd asked her to maintain their status quo at work and to keep their time together strictly confidential. She'd agreed without pause. No one was going to accuse her of trading on a relationship with a man to get ahead in her career. Besides, there was something really alluring about clandestine meetings with the super sexy Marcello.

She loved talking to him on the phone and knowing that they were carrying on a conversation on a whole level that the people around them knew nothing about. Then he had to go away on a business trip and she missed him like crazy. He only called once and it was a short conversation. It had to be...she'd been at work.

They had plans to eat out the night after he got back, but when he came to pick her up, she had made dinner. She wanted time with him, to be completely natural together and the only way for that to happen was behind closed doors.

He sniffed appreciatively when she ushered him inside. "It smells so good, I almost want to beg to stay in and have leftovers."

"We are staying in, only they aren't leftovers. I made dinner."

"Is it a special occasion?"

"I thought I could teach you how to play Golf."

His brow drew together in puzzlement as he looked around the cottage's small living room. "I am already a competent golfer."

She laughed at his incomprehension. "It's a card game and one of the few that is as much fun with two people as four."

"Oh. *Cards*?"

"I thought you might be happier eating in and relaxing than going out to a restaurant, but if you'd rather...I can just wrap dinner up and get my coat."

"Not at all. I have never had a woman cook for me."

"Not even your wife?"

He rarely mentioned Bianca, but she knew he'd married young and his wife had died in a tragic accident.

"To my knowledge, Bianca did not know how to cook."

"Was she a princess?"

"To me? Yes, but she was not born to royalty. She was from a very wealthy Sicilian family. Her mother was my mother's best friend."

"It sounds like a match made in heaven."

"It was, but I lived in hell on earth when she died."

Why that should hurt so much to hear, she didn't know, but she did realize it wasn't all pain on his behalf. "I'm sorry."

"Thank you. They say time heals all wounds."

"I don't know about healing, but it does dull the pain…or makes it easier to cope with."

"Are you talking about Ray here?"

"No."

"Then what?"

Funny, how she'd told him so much about herself, but never about her corrected spinal deformity. It was too painful to talk about even now. The wounds it had visited on her life were too deep to expose to him or anyone else, for that matter.

She'd never told anyone about her decision not to have children because of it, or how alienated she'd felt from the world around her and even from her own body. Her brace had acted as a barrier between her and the sensation of touch for thirteen years. It had also distorted her view of her body. How could she explain what it was like to look into the mirror and see a figure that was defined by an expensive plastic encasement? She could not even be sure whether the curves were hers, or the result of the brace.

When she'd finally stopped wearing it, she had been afraid her body would change back, that her spine would curve once again and that the female curves she saw in the mirror would disappear now that their plastic encasement was gone. She'd been twenty-one before she'd finally decided her body really was hers again.

And even then, she often saw the brace when she looked in the mirror, rather than the actual woman looking back at her.

She shrugged. "Everyone has pain in their lives, Marcello. I'm no different, but it doesn't matter. I didn't ask you about Bianca to hurt you."

He touched her hand—nothing sexy, just a small brushing of their fingers—but her entire body felt like it had been electrified. "You did not. You never dig for juicy details or push me to bare my emotions. I appreciate that."

She laughed. "You would. The only person I know who is more private about their feelings than myself, is you."

"I would not have guessed you were such a private person at first."

"Protective persona. Most of us have them."

"Not my brothers. What you see is what you get with them."

"Are you sure about that? I bet even your father has an image he allows the rest of the world to see that protects the man behind his skin…the man who isn't a king."

"There, I know you are wrong. King Vincente is exactly as he appears to be. A sovereign to the marrow of his bones."

"Or he's just very adept at hiding any weakness, even from the people he loves the most."

"Trust me, his weaknesses are in no way hidden."

She had a hard time believing the son could be so very different from the father, but she didn't know either well enough to argue the point. "Whatever you say."

"I say that I am very appreciative that you chose to cook for me."

She smiled and led him to the small dining room, where she'd set the table with candles and her best dishes.

"It looks like a scene set for seduction."

"Maybe it is," she joked.

He turned to face her and put his hand on her face, the warm fingers sending more tingles of sensation zinging through her body. "I would not mind."

"I was only kidding."

"I am not."

"Um…maybe you had better sit down."

He sat and he said nothing more, but he kept giving her looks throughout dinner that were as effective as any caress.

Afterward, they took dessert, a homemade lemon sorbet, into the living room.

He pulled her to the sofa beside him, their hips touching. "Dinner was fantastic. Thank you, *cara*."

"You…you're welcome."

"I'm going to kiss you now."

"I…"

"Do you mind?"

"No." This was what she had wanted when she invited him to stay in for dinner, but when it came to the sticking point, she was nervous.

What if he found her as big a dud as Ray had done?

Marcello followed through on his promise to kiss her with a thoroughness that had her clinging to his shoulders while desire pooled low in her belly. He tasted like the lemon sorbet and sexy, delectable male. It was so different than when Ray had kissed her. With Marcello, she just wanted more and more and more. And he gave it to her, exploring her mouth with his tongue and letting her return the favor.

Finally he ended the kiss with a series of gentle pecks on her swollen lips. He lifted his head. "That went well, *cara*. I think we should do it again."

She nodded, incapable of speech.

Then he put his hands on her waist and brushed his thumbs up and down over her rib cage. "But this time, I want you sitting on my lap."

He couldn't know it, but that kind of touch was incredibly foreign to her. She'd developed habits as a child that kept people at a distance physically. Unconsciously she'd avoided Ray's touch as well. And when they did neck, he'd had a tendency to go straight for certain body parts. She hadn't enjoyed his caresses all that much and had assumed it was because she just wasn't very sexual. She now realized she'd been absolutely, terribly…no, *wonderfully* wrong.

Because she was reacting to Marcello's touch like a woman who had been in a desert her whole life and was just now stumbling on the Lake Erie of sensation. And in many ways, it was true.

Ray had not had the water she needed, but she felt drenched by emotions from Marcello's touch.

She scooted into his lap, loving the feel of his hard thighs below her. His hands moved around to caress her back with an erotic sweeping motion that made her tremble.

"You're very good at this."

He laughed and pressed his lips to hers again.

His hands moved all over her body in gentle, brushing strokes that made her feel like he was trying to see her with his hands. It was amazing and she grew scorching hot as her breasts swelled inside her lacy bra cups and the place between her legs grew damp and achingly swollen.

He stopped kissing her. "Don't you want to touch me?"

"Huh…what?" she asked, dazed by the deep, dark cravings rolling through her.

"Your hands are clenched at your sides."

"Oh, I don't mean them to be." And to prove she meant what she said, she splayed her fingers across his chest.

Heat emanated from him to her fingertips, even through his clothes. "I want to feel your skin."

"Then do it. I am not going to turn down any way you want to touch me, Danette."

There was something important in that reassurance, but she couldn't work it out in her head right now.

She unbuttoned his shirt with shaking hands and touched him with those same trembling fingers. She'd never felt this way touching Ray, like she was on a very important journey of discovery. One that would kill her if she didn't take it.

She explored Marcello's chest with total concentration given to every nuance of feeling, every detail of his masculine build her fingertips encountered. His muscles made ridges under his bronzed skin. The dark, curling hair that covered his chest and disappeared in an enticing V into his pants was surprisingly soft to the touch. Shouldn't male hair be coarse and, well…*manly*? But it felt so sexy, so incredible…and the skin beneath it was so warm. It was like touching heated satin.

She traced each ridge and she pressed her fingertip into his belly button while her thumb brushed the hair-roughened skin below it.

He groaned. "*Cara*, you are playing with fire there."

He *was* fire…all elemental heat. Everything a man should be for a woman.

Her hands swept up his torso, stopping at his rigid male nipples. "You are so different from me," she breathed.

He choked out a laugh. "You talk like you've never touched a man before."

"I haven't. Not like this."

His hands froze in the act of pushing her top up to expose her skin to his heated gaze.

"What are you saying? *Tesoro*, you cannot be a virgin. I do not believe it."

She stared at him, and then blinked, trying to make sense of his shock. "Why not? I told you that Ray was not my lover."

"But surely there have been other men."

"No."

"But American girls date in high school and college. Everyone knows this to be true."

"This one didn't." The passion clouding her brain began to fade. "I never had a boyfriend."

"Why not? Were your parents too protective?"

"You could say that." And she hadn't wanted to date, either. She didn't like explaining about the brace and no way would she have let a boy touch her and touch it. She couldn't stand being so exposed.

Marcello moved back from her, gently removing her hands from his body. "This is not right. I thought you were a woman of experience. I cannot take your innocence."

No, he couldn't mean it. This wasn't some Victorian tragedy. She was a modern woman, and perhaps waiting for marriage was something she'd thought at one time she would do, but she didn't feel that way right now. She didn't want any other man to be her first.

Only this one.

"But I can *give* it to you."

"I am not looking for marriage here. I do not want a long-term relationship."

"I'm not looking for marriage, either." She'd missed out on so much, the dating, the furtive moments of passion teenagers share, the love affairs in college. "I want to experience it all with you, Marcello. I trust you."

"But you are a virgin. You should wait until you get married."

"I want you to be my first man. I've never felt this kind of desire before and I'm afraid I'll never feel this way again. I sure didn't with Ray."

"He was a creep."

"Yes, but you're not. I know you won't hurt me…I know you can make it special my first time."

"You know this, huh?"

"You may not be the playboy the media paints you, but you're experienced enough to know what you're doing. You make me crazy just being with you." She didn't want to beg, but she was close. "If you want me, too…at least a little…I want you to be my first lover."

"I want you a great deal more than a little," he growled, his eyes shooting blue flame at her. The hottest kind of flame and she felt singed to the depths of her soul.

"I'm glad, Marcello, because I want you a lot, too."

"Our relationship remains strictly private. I will not allow the media into my personal life, which means others cannot know about us, either."

"I don't have a problem with that."

Danette abruptly returned to the present. She *hadn't* had a problem with the secrecy then….but this was now and she did have a problem with it. A big problem. She just wasn't sure what she could do about it.

If anything.

She loved him and that love demanded a role in his life that stretched beyond a secret affair. Maybe if she told him her feelings he would acknowledge his own and they could move to the next step in their relationship.

It wasn't that she thought he lacked confidence. If he knew he loved her, he would say so, but his heart was locked up tight behind the wall he'd built after Bianca's death. Danette had managed to knock out chinks here and there, evidenced by the fact that their relationship had lasted so long and how much time they spent together doing stuff besides making love.

While he refused to tell her how many women had come before her, he had let slip that none of them had lasted beyond a very brief liaison. He had been with her for six months and made no indications he was even thinking about moving on.

There was also the fact that he frequently made love to her without protection. He'd done so again the night before.

The first time it had happened, she'd been shocked by her response. Since she had decided as a teenager not to have children and risk passing on her spinal deformity, she should have been really upset by his lapse. But her first reaction to the realization he'd forgotten the condom had not been dismay. Far from it: she'd had a piercingly sweet image of a little boy with her eyes and Marcello's smile.

She had experienced a craving for that child that was so great, it had been a physical pain in her chest.

Nevertheless, she'd brought up the option of her going on the pill, but Marcello had been adamant it was not necessary. He knew from one of the many discussions they had on every topic under the sun that she had some family history of breast cancer, and therefore concerned about the possible increased risk from long-term use of the pill.

She'd agreed to allow him to continue to be responsible for the birth control and had not raised the issue again the next time he forgot. Instead she'd researched the probability of passing her severe idiomatic juvenile scoliosis onto her children. She'd discovered that, far from what she'd feared, there was actually no known genetic predisposition for what had happened to her.

She couldn't dismiss the very real fact that her mother had been afflicted with a less severe case. Even so, she'd all but convinced herself it was a risk worth taking. She refused to allow her childhood disease and what it represented to stand between her and Marcello.

Right now, she had to weigh the fact that he talked like the future was uncertain for them against the fact that he forgot to use birth control almost as often as he remembered. No man took that many risks with pregnancy when he hated the idea of spending his future with the woman involved.

Marcello wasn't the irresponsible kind. If she got pregnant, she knew he'd want to marry her. He had a strong sense of moral and family responsibility. Both of which would require that his child not be born illegitimate. In turn, that *must* mean he was considering a future with her, even if he was leery about admitting it to her, or even to himself.

It might be a subconscious thing on his part, but his actions spoke loud and clear about where he was at with her emotionally. At least she hoped they did. No amount of wishful surmising on her part could replace hearing the words from his lips.

His wife's death had devastated him. She'd quickly realized that he didn't want to risk that kind of pain again, but she could have told him that love did not respect the fear of being hurt.

Just look at her. She had come to Italy licking her wounds. She'd been grateful for the job that Angelo had gotten her so that she could get away from her memories. And she'd been convinced that the last thing she would allow herself to do was to get embroiled in another relationship. Only, that was exactly what she had done and she'd gotten in deeper with Marcello after two weeks than she had in months with Ray.

She'd come to Marcello a virgin and she knew that was as important to him as it was to her.

Part of her, deep down, wished she would just get pregnant and then neither of them would have a choice about secrecy or the rest of it anymore. But part of her was frightened by the prospect of pregnancy, and a much bigger part needed him to come to terms with his feelings for her on his own. She wanted him to acknowledge he cared about her and she needed to know that for sure, too. Not just hope and guess at it.

Maybe telling him that she loved him would open another chink in the wall around his heart…the most important one.

She hoped so, because if it didn't, she'd didn't know what she would do.

Later that day when he came into her office to ask for her report on the Cordoba project, when he could have requested the information through his assistant, that hope blossomed.

CHAPTER FOUR

MARCELLO walked into Danette's office and felt like he'd been hit in the chest with a polo mallet when she gave him that smile she reserved especially for him.

Her amber eyes glowed golden with welcome and his body reacted as if it had been months, not hours, since he had last buried himself inside her. He became instantly hard—to the point of pain. He found himself pushing the door shut behind him, though that was probably the last thing he should do.

"I have the report for you right here." She tucked her light brown hair behind her ear with a flirtatious wink. "That is what you came for, isn't it?"

The significant look she gave the shut door belied the innocence of her words and he grinned in response. He couldn't help it. Like all of his reactions to her from the moment he had first seen her, it was beyond his usually formidable control. He had never looked to one of his employees for friendship, much less an affair and he had fought his feelings for her for four months. But in the end…he had lost.

He hadn't been able to dismiss the cravings for her body and that particular sweet smile he'd never seen her give anyone else. It was a craving that grew when fed, he'd discovered, rather than diminishing. Which put it in the realm of an addiction he could not kick. As much as he hated the vulnerability such an addiction spawned, he had learned that to give into it brought its own reward. The more time he spent with her, the more at peace he felt, and after making love was the best of all.

Even though he knew he should be opening that door and getting down to business, not putting the anonymity of their affair at risk, he was powerless to do so. His gaze skimmed her slight figure as his libido heated to volcanic levels and he acknowledged there was a big difference between knowing what he should do and being able to do it.

"That is the excuse I gave my assistant, yes."

"Perhaps there was something else you wanted from me?" she asked in a come-hither voice that went straight to his already throbbing groin.

That overtly flirtatious manner and her American frankness had fooled him into believing she was a much more experienced woman than she was for the first months of their association. Right up until he'd touched her with intent for the first time and found out she was a virgin, and an incredibly innocent one at that. She'd known almost nothing of passion.

He'd seen too late that for all her appearance of outgoing friendliness, she was actually rather shy. She knew even less of men than she did of physical desire. And he had shamelessly taken advantage of her willingness to learn with him.

He'd been careful to spell out the parameters of their affair, though. She'd deserved to know where they were headed—to bed—and where they were not going—

down the aisle toward matrimony. He'd been very clear. No commitments. No permanent ties. Absolute secrecy.

And she had still welcomed him with an innocent but generous passion that left him shaking.

She'd never brought up the other parameters of their affair and he had to assume she understood their relationship was not a permanent one, but she had become unhappy with the need for secrecy. She'd been hurt by that picture in the tabloid and he hated knowing that, but if the media became aware of her existence in his life, she would be at risk of a lot more hurt and continuous harassment.

Although he understood her current feelings, he could not give into them. It was imperative he remain strong for both of their sakes. He hated having his real private life the focus of public cynosure. He'd had enough of that with his marriage. The press had hounded him and Bianca from the very first. No doubt contributing to what came later. They'd married young and that alone had been newsworthy…to some. Many had assumed she was pregnant, but she hadn't been.

Then, when two years went by and no pregnancy showed on the horizon, speculation started. It was a mere reflection of the concerns he and Bianca shared in the privacy of their bedroom. Because they'd done nothing to prevent pregnancy from their wedding night onward. She had been the first one to undergo tests, but her reproductive system was functioning normally.

He'd offered to have the tests taken as well, never dreaming the doctor would discover a really low sperm count. He would never forget the chilling humiliation when one of the scandal rags had gotten wind of his near sterility. They had run the story and others had picked it up until he and his wife could not go out in public without being asked if they planned to adopt, try IVF or worse.

Bianca had said it didn't matter, but Marcello had seen her pain when her friends fell pregnant and she did not. He had seen the longing in her eyes when she held her cousins' babies, and he'd listened to her cry at night in their bathroom when she thought he was sleeping.

He felt like his manhood had been stripped away from him. Having it happen in the public eye had been ten times worse. He would never willingly go through that again.

"Marcello?" Danette asked, her expression concerned.

He forced the bleak thoughts from his mind and focused on the situation at hand. "There is definitely something else you can give me." It was more than her body and her desire that he was talking about. Making love to Danette banished the ghosts of the past...for a little while.

"Something more important than the report?" she asked with a vulnerability he wished he couldn't see.

She wanted confirmation that she was more important to him than the work she did for him, but if he gave it to her, then he would be implying a depth to their relationship he had been careful to refrain from establishing. He couldn't do that. It wouldn't be fair. But from the look in her lovely amber eyes, he knew not to do so wasn't being fair to her, either.

She deserved better than what he could give her. She deserved a man who could and would date her openly, one who could give her a future with a complete family. Not a playboy prince who could offer her great sex and companionship only when it was out of the public eye— and no future.

Knowing what she deserved didn't change his need for her, though. Marcello was not about to give her up. Not yet.

She added too much to his life.

One day, she would move on, but until then, he would give her all that he could and take all she was willing to offer.

"It certainly feels more urgent," he compromised.

It appeased her and she smiled again, this time her eyes going dark with a familiar fire. "What could it be then?"

He leaned back against the door, his legs spread slightly, his body telling her he wasn't going anywhere. "Come here and I'll show you."

"I don't think so." She cocked her head to one side and looked at him. "You look dangerous."

"And you feel safe with the desk between us?"

She shrugged, but the look she gave him from between her lashes was pure provocation. "Maybe. I guess that all depends on how much energy you're willing to expend."

He pushed away from the door and stalked over to her, his body thrumming with the incredible sexual excitement only she generated in him. When he reached her, she scooted back in her chair, but the primal man inside him was not about to let his prize retreat.

Marcello reached out with lightning quick movements to grab Danette's shoulders and prevent her withdrawal. Suddenly their playful banter was overshadowed by a dark, perilous desire he had never unleashed in the office before.

She gasped. "Marcello, what are you *doing*?"

She'd been playing. Flirting in a way she knew drove him crazy, but never in a million years had she expected him to take her up on it within the hallowed walls of Scorsolini Shipping.

He pulled her from the chair. "I want you, Danette. Now."

"Wh—"

His mouth slammed down on hers with primitive passion, his intent unmistakable.

The urbane and sophisticated playboy everyone else saw when they looked at him was gone. In his place was a man of earthy passion and raw masculinity that only she ever saw and she found totally irresistible.

The kiss went incendiary immediately. His lips sucked on hers, his tongue demanded entrance into her mouth, and his teeth nipped at her bottom lip. She gave back as good as she got, her tongue tangling with his in delicious, erotic abandon. She couldn't get enough. Her brain was barely functioning when he moved his mouth along her jaw to wreak havoc on the sensitive areas he knew so well.

"*Here*?" she whispered with her last grasp at rational thought. "You want to make love here?"

His answer was to growl like some primitive animal, slide his hand possessively down over the curve of her breast and squeeze. She moaned.

"Shh…*amante*, you must be silent."

"I can't…"

"You can and you will," he promised in a shadowy drawl and then challenged that assumption with sensual caresses that made her body swell with pleasure.

She tugged at his tie, undoing it and the buttons of his shirt with impatient fingers. She peeled the fabric away to reveal the hair-roughened contours of his chest and abdomen. She curled her fingers in it reflexively and the breath stilled in her chest at the sight of her fingers on his skin.

He was such a beautiful, beautiful man.

He made a harsh sound and then whispered, "Yes, just like that, Danette *mia*. Give me your passion, *amante*."

She leaned forward and took his small, rigid nipple between her teeth and nipped, then licked it to soothe the sting before sucking it into her mouth as she knew he liked.

His body jerked and he made a muted sound of passion before yanking her blouse up to expose her bra clad breasts. One flick of his fingers and the front clasp came apart and then his hands were on her, tormenting her with the kind of caresses that would bring her to the brink of climax before he ever touched her most intimate flesh.

His hands went everywhere, rubbing her back, kneading her bottom and sliding under her skirt with a lack of finesse that said better than anything else could have how out of control he really was. His big frame shuddered when she attacked his belt buckle and then the zipper on his slacks.

She slid it down with agonizing slowness, not wanting to hurt the flesh straining against it and reveling in the anticipation of what she would reveal. She pushed his waistband down, carefully pulling the elastic of his shorts over his pulsing, erect flesh. His rigid length sprang out to greet her. Curling her fingers around his satin hardness, she squeezed possessively.

"Yes, yours," he said, showing he knew exactly what she was thinking.

Then he picked her up by the waist and sat her on the edge of her desk, moving between her legs boldly so that her thighs were parted wide and left open to him.

She'd worn stockings like she always did and the fragile silk of her panties proved no barrier to his touch. He tore them from her body with primitive violence that sent a burst of humid warmth through her secret place.

He cupped her, one long finger sliding inside. "Mine."

"Yesss…" she hissed.

Then he was there, exactly where she most needed him to be, and she whimpered with the exquisite pleasure of it. He was big and she spread her legs wider to accommodate him, wrapping her calves around his lean waist. He grabbed her hips and pressed inexorably forward, his hardness stretching her almost unbearably, but feeling so right and so good that tears of intense desire burned her eyes.

"You fit me so perfectly," he whispered roughly into her hair, and thrust in to the hilt.

She couldn't reply. Her throat was too tight with the need to cry out her pleasure and the effort it took to suppress those cries.

She buried her face in his neck, biting her lips together to hold back the sounds as he thrust against her with powerful movements that shook her whole body. The pleasure spun tight and high inside of her instantly and she exploded in rapturous bliss after only a few body-racking thrusts. Her flesh convulsed around him, her entire being shuddering with her culmination.

His grip on her hips tightened bruisingly and he bit back a growl as his body went stiff against hers and he released his pleasure inside of her. They remained locked in primal ecstasy for what could have been mere seconds or much longer. Time meant nothing on that plane of existence. Only sensation mattered and it was so overwhelming, her head spun in a dizzy black void.

Even when the pleasure waned, he did not move and neither did she. She was in too much shock. She couldn't believe they had made love *in her office*. Her door didn't even have a lock, for goodness' sake. It went against everything he preached about keeping their private association private. The risk of exposure was huge and yet, he had not even hesitated.

The fact that his need for her was so great made her feel warm deep down inside. That *had* to mean something.

"I cannot believe we just did that," he said mirroring her thoughts.

"You started it."

He laughed against her temple before turning her face up for a tender kiss of soul-stirring proportions. "You provoked me, *amante,* do not try to deny it. You know I find you irresistible."

"I didn't mean to provoke *this*." And she hadn't. It would never have occurred to her to try to tease him into making love in the office.

She felt shattered by having fallen into it so completely herself. Was she a complete wanton, that the thought of her office door's inability to lock hadn't even entered her mind until afterward? Or depraved even?

"No doubt," he mused against her face as he pressed another small kiss to her temple. "You are too innocent to take such an encounter in your stride."

"And you are not?" she asked, the sensation of his body still locked to hers suddenly making her feel incredibly vulnerable.

"I left my rose-colored glasses of innocence behind me long ago, but if you are wondering if sex in the office is a norm for me, let me assure you that it is not."

For some reason, that made her feel better than it

should. His past shouldn't matter, but knowing he broke his own rules for her did.

He pulled out of her, but did not move so she could close her legs. Instead he used tissues from the dispenser on her desk to clean her up and she found that act every bit as intimate as the one they had just performed and a lot more embarrassing.

"Marcello…"

"This will make it more comfortable for you."

She didn't know what else to say, so she choked out an uncomfortable, "Thank you."

His blue gaze flicked to her face and he shook his head. "How can you blush now, when seconds ago you were receiving me into your body with a passion that could burn the sun?"

The heat of her blush intensified and she bit her lip. When he continued to look at her inquiringly, she admitted, "When you touch me, you make me forget everything else."

He continued to care for her, his attention thorough. "I am touching you now."

"It's not the same."

"No, it is not, but my body does not seem to know that."

She looked down and realized that his arousal was growing again.

"You can't want…not again!"

"I want. Do not mistake it…but I will not take again. Not here. I should not have kissed you that first time. I cannot believe we did this in your office. It was not my brightest moment."

"You make it sound like you regret making love to me." And while she agreed that their venue had not been as private as she would have liked, that implication still hurt.

After all, nothing bad had happened.

"I could never regret the kind of pleasure I find in your body."

"Good. Because I don't regret it, either."

He finished what he was doing and finally stepped back so she could bring her legs together.

He buttoned his shirt and tucked it into his slacks with quick, efficient movements. "You said that the first time we made love. Do you remember?"

"How could I forget?" she asked as she redid her bra and blouse, impatient to be put back together now that the passion no longer fogged her brain and she was all too aware of the risk of someone knocking on her office door.

"I was your first lover and you did not regret that, even though I could not make the promises that a virgin should expect her first lover to make." He spoke while retying his tie and did not look at her.

"Are we going to get into that again?" Once had been plenty for her.

He sighed, the sound odd considering what they'd just been doing. "There is no need."

"Right." Besides, promises or no promises, he'd shown her in many ways that she was special to him. She finished dressing, ruefully tossing her panties in the trash when she saw they could never be worn again. "Will I see you tonight?"

He tugged his tie into place and finger combed his hair, leaving his appearance as pristine and businesslike as before. "I have plans this evening."

"Business plans?" she asked.

"Does it matter?"

She frowned. "After our discussion last night, do you have to ask?"

He shook his head with impatience. "I am not going out with another woman."

"So, it *is* business."

He merely shrugged, which was not an answer. She was preparing to press for one when he picked her panties up out of the trash.

"What are you doing? Don't tell me you want a souvenir."

"Do not be crude."

"Um…I'm not the one who just grabbed torn underwear from the circular file." But she was the one blushing about it. Aargh! She really wasn't in his league.

"I do not wish to leave them here for the cleaning crew to find. It could cause speculation."

"And you don't think the closed door will do that?"

"There are many reasons besides having wild, urgent sex on a desk to close an office door when I am meeting with an employee, but there are no reasons *but* sex to explain ripped lingerie in the waste bin."

"I see. And of course it would be an absolute tragedy if someone were to guess that you'd been making love with me."

It was his turn to frown. "We have been over this."

"Yes."

He pulled her to him, but she didn't melt against him like she normally did.

He sighed again. "Believe it, or not, but I am protecting you as much as I am protecting myself. You do not know how vicious the scandal rags can be."

Remembering the stories her former boyfriend had

helped to dish up on her friend Tara and Angelo Gordon, she shook her head. "You're wrong. I do know. I'm just not as scared of it as you are."

She also remembered the way that Angelo had responded to the ugly stories. He had stood beside Tara, proud to be her lover. But then Angelo had wanted to marry Tara.

Marcello looked supremely offended. "I am not afraid."

"Whatever you say."

"Are you trying to pick an argument?" he asked in a tone that implied he couldn't believe she'd want to after what they had just done.

And she didn't. Not really. "No."

He picked up the report from the corner of her desk. "I must go."

"Yes."

"I do not like to see you like this."

"Like what?" Like she'd just been made love to and was still reeling from the aftereffects?

"Your sparkle is missing."

She didn't know what he was talking about. "I'm in work mode. I don't sparkle at work."

"This is not true. It was the life blazing from your golden eyes that first caught my interest."

"Well, we both know it wasn't my body," she said in a poor attempt at a joke. Her curves were slight and her face was average…it still shocked her Marcello had chosen her for his lover, secret or not.

"Your body is perfect, or is it not obvious I think this?"

It *was* obvious. The one thing she knew with total certainty was that he found her irresistibly sexually attractive. She didn't understand it and she wasn't sure that was enough anymore.

If she couldn't convince herself that he cared, at least a little, she'd fall into complete despair.

"If you don't leave, there is going to be speculation about my job performance or lack thereof because of that shut door."

He nodded, his eyes probing hers as if looking for answers. She had none for him. At least not right now…not here.

He stopped at the door. "I could come by later tonight."

His offer shouldn't have made her spirits lift, but even though it was such a small concession, it did.

"If you like."

"I do like. I enjoy sleeping with you in my arms."

"Even when we don't make love?" But she knew the answer to that. He spent as many nights during her monthly as he did when she was available sexually.

"Even then, but tonight, there will be no barriers," he said, showing that once again his mind was traveling the same path as hers.

Didn't that kind of intimacy of thought mean something?

She could only pray it did because if she really was just a body in his bed, she didn't think she'd survive the pain of that kind of reality.

CHAPTER FIVE

LIZZY came by Danette's office later that afternoon to ask if she wanted to go out to dinner to celebrate finishing the Cordoba project.

Danette accepted without hesitation. "That sounds terrific."

And much better than spending another evening alone wondering what Marcello was doing that he couldn't be with her.

"Where do you want to eat?"

"You choose."

"No way. This is your celebration."

She named a restaurant that was one of her favorites. Marcello had introduced it to her. It was a small eatery run by a local family and the food was superb. Its ambience was hardly what a prince was used to and she'd often wondered if he took her more for the relative privacy it offered than even the excellent food. It definitely wasn't the type of place where the paparazzi hung out to catch glimpses of the newsworthy.

If they tried, she had no doubt that Giuseppe, the owner, would have tossed them out with a few choice words.

When she arrived, she asked Giuseppe if Lizzy had already arrived.

"You are not eating with Principe Tomasso tonight?" he asked instead of answering.

"No."

He frowned, his expression an odd one she could not decipher. If she didn't know better, she'd think the older Sicilian man looked worried about something, but what there was to worry about in her eating dinner with Lizzy, she couldn't imagine.

But all he said was, "Your friends, they are this way."

He led her to a table in the back and it was only as they reached it that the import of Giuseppe's words hit her. Because Lizzy was not the only person at the table. Her current boyfriend and Ramon from the sales department at Scorsolini Shipping were both sitting there, too.

Ramon had worked with her on several aspects of the Cordoba project. Maybe that was why he was there, maybe he wanted to celebrate too, but more likely Lizzy was playing matchmaker. If that were the case, Danette was going to cheerfully strangle her friend.

However, she pasted a smile on her face when Ramon hopped up to help her into her chair. "Thank you."

"It is my pleasure. I am glad you finally agreed to see me outside of work."

Lizzy flushed guiltily and Danette almost said she hadn't agreed to any such thing, but refused to deal that kind of blow to the man's ego. It wasn't his fault Lizzy was playing games Danette did not want to engage in. Ramon had never been anything but kind to her, even if he was a hopeless flirt and had a reputation for dating more women than most. And really, she couldn't be too angry with Lizzy, either. The other woman didn't know Danette was already in a relationship, but she did know Danette didn't want to date Ramon.

She shrugged. "Blame Lizzy." She knew she did, and the look she gave the other American woman said so.

Lizzy just grinned back, all evidence of guilt gone, her expression now full of satisfaction in a plan well executed.

They were eating their salad and bread, Ramon at his charming best, which Danette had to admit was likable, when she felt a tingling sensation in the back of her neck. Still smiling from something Ramon had said, she looked around, trying to account for it. Her breath stilled in shock when she saw Marcello with three other people.

Danette recognized all of them from photos she'd seen in the media. The older woman, with hair the same golden-brown as Marcello's and a face that was almost painfully beautiful, was his mother. The man next to Marcello was his older brother, Principe Tomasso Scorsolini, and the woman glowing with happiness at his side was Tomasso's new fiancée, Maggie Thomson.

So, *not* business. Family. And he had clearly not wanted to introduce her to them. She understood keeping their relationship hidden from the public eye, she really did. She might not like it, but she could not fault his reasoning for it. However, why did she have to be kept a secret from his family as well? Surely none of them would leak anything to the press.

He must have felt her eyes on him because he turned and their gazes met across the small but crowded restaurant. His eyes widened fractionally and then narrowed before his mother said something to him and he turned away to speak to her, giving no indication of acknowledgment to Danette.

It sliced through her heart like a jagged blade and she touched her chest, feeling like there should be an open wound there.

"Isn't that the big boss?" Lizzy demanded in an awed whisper. "The prince himself?"

Ramon turned and he studied the newcomers. "Yes, it is."

Giuseppe was now leading the foursome to a table that would take Marcello's party right by where Danette sat.

She felt like she couldn't breathe. She didn't know what she would do if he walked right by without even acknowledging her. At least at work, he always extended the courtesy of recognizing her presence…just as he did all the employees he knew by name.

She was saved from finding out when Ramon stood up with a smile, his hand extended to Marcello. The men greeted one another. Then Marcello introduced all of them to his family…as employees of Scorsolini Shipping.

He did not linger over his introduction of her, not even by a millisecond, and there could be no indication to his family that she was special to him in any way. Which was exactly what she should have expected, but she still felt horribly slighted. It hurt, and it didn't matter that he had not really betrayed her or that he was acting only as he had always said he would.

Her heart was tight with pain and the rest of her felt numb.

She said something in response to the introductions,

though she had no idea what. Her brain wasn't functioning all that well. Marcello's eyes narrowed, and she wondered if she'd said something wrong, but no one else reacted strangely. So, it must have been okay.

Conversation flowed back and forth, but none of it penetrated the pain imploding inside her.

Lizzy made a comment and they laughed, but they were looking at Danette and she realized she'd missed something.

Lizzy grinned. "Her head's in the clouds. She just finished an important project and she put so much into it, I think she frazzled her brain."

"And here I had hoped it was that she was overawed because she finally agreed to go out with me," Ramon said with such blatant humor that even Danette's lips curved in a tiny smile.

Everyone else laughed out loud…except Marcello.

For the space of a single heartbeat his glare could have singed concrete, but then a mask of imperturbability settled over his face.

"You see, Marcello? This is what you should be doing, my son."

"And what is that, Mama?"

"Like these young men, you should be dating some nice girl, but it is always work, work, work with you. The hours he puts in." She shook her head. "*Ai, ai, ai.* He thinks of nothing but business. And here we see there are plenty of lovely young women who work for you that you could socialize with."

"I do not make it a habit to date employees," he said with a perfectly straight face.

Danette gasped, her face stinging with heat as if it had been struck.

His look of concern lasted longer than the glare, but she ignored it. So, he didn't date employees? What was their relationship then, a series of clandestine *meetings*? Even as she asked herself the question, her heart knew the answer.

That was exactly what they had. A series of secret trysts that meant nothing more to him than a one-night stand. They couldn't and have him deny her to his family so completely.

"I am glad you do not expect your employees to adhere to that principle," Ramon said with a smile for Danette.

Lizzy and her date chimed in and Marcello merely shrugged, but there was something feral in the cobalt-blue gaze he fixed on Ramon.

Danette could not leave it there. Would not do so…it wasn't right. "So, you *never* date employees?" she asked with a voice that sounded to her like shattered glass.

"I keep my private life private," he said by way of a nonanswer.

"There aren't any women at Scorsolini Shipping glamorous enough for the prince," Lizzy said cheekily. "I've seen pictures of the women he dates. They're cover model types for sure. I mean if they ended up married, she'd be a princess wouldn't she? Someone like Miss Thompson here fits the bill." She indicated Prince Tomasso's perfectly groomed and thoroughly lovely fiancée with a nod of her head. "But I can't see any of the women at Scorsolini shipping being that kind of glamour material."

Maggie Thompson made a strange sound.

Prince Tomasso smiled at her. "I told you that you are my perfect mate."

Lizzy's eyes went all dreamy. "Isn't that romantic?" she asked the table in general.

"Very," Danette said, feeling as far from romantic herself as it was possible to get. "No doubt if Marcello was dating a cover model or someone as lovely as the soon-to-be princess, he wouldn't be such a stickler for privacy."

Her words held a message for him that no one else would get, but it was only after speaking that she realized she'd used his first name. While he encouraged a less formal address amongst his employees than "Your Highness", she still should have called him Signor Scorsolini.

She didn't know if the anger tightening his jaw was for her slip or her implication.

"Are you kidding?" Lizzy demanded, filling the awkward silence. "There wasn't anything private about the picture of Signor Scorsolini dancing with that gorgeous blonde at his father's birthday party. Oooh, la, la. What a couple." She waggled her eyebrows dramatically, making everyone laugh again.

"She was only one of many gorgeous creatures he danced with that night," Maggie Thomson said, her smile wide. "I don't mind telling you, I was glad he was there to draw some of the attention away from Tomasso."

"I live to serve," Marcello said with a forced facetiousness she doubted anyone else noticed was not entirely natural.

Danette wasn't feeling humorous, either. She cocked her head to one side and examined his brother. In many ways the two men looked alike. They were both tall and shared the same cobalt-blue eyes, though Marcello's skin was darker. His hair was lighter, but both men wore it a little long and had matching widow's peaks. The expression of supreme male confidence they wore was identical, too.

"Tell me something, Prince Tomasso, if you don't mind."

Sliding an arm around his fiancée's waist, he smiled at Danette. "What would you like to know?"

"How do you manage to balance your princely duty to socialize with your personal life? For example, could you dance with one woman as your brother did, while wooing your fiancée, persuading her you cared about her?"

"Ah, you must remember, my brother is smart enough not to have told any woman such a thing, so the question doesn't arise in his case. He's very adept at juggling excess amounts of female attention. But in answer to your question, Maggie would brain me if I danced with another woman the way my brother danced at our father's party. And rightly so. I prefer to keep my head in one piece and therefore would not risk it, no."

Everyone laughed while Danette felt the blood draining from her face. *The way that Marcello had danced with the other women*...he hadn't just been putting on a front. He'd been enjoying himself, playing the field. Maybe even looking for her replacement. Okay, so it was probable he hadn't slept with any of them, but she still felt a holocaust of pain where her heart should be.

Her eyes met Marcello's and she knew that right that second, all the pain she was feeling was there for him to see.

He cursed, shocking everyone around them and Prince Tomasso said, "What's the matter?"

"I did not dance like a damned gigolo."

"I never said you did. You merely acted like the single man you are and had a lot of fun doing it. I, however, am content to be attached." And the look he gave Maggie left no one at the table, or standing beside it, in any doubt how very sincerely he felt those words.

Tears burned the back of Danette's eyes and she blinked furiously to get rid of them. Marcello looked livid. She couldn't imagine why. His brother only spoke the truth after all.

Lizzy sighed, the dreamy look back. "That's just so sweet."

Her date grinned. "I can be just as sweet, do you doubt it?"

She laughed. "Of course not. I wouldn't be here with you otherwise."

"We shouldn't keep you from your table any longer," Danette said to Marcello through stiff lips, not meeting his eyes.

She wanted them gone and did not care if she wasn't at her subtle best in achieving that goal. As it was, she had no idea how she was going to hold it together for the remainder of dinner. But she would somehow. She wasn't making an idiot of herself in public over a relationship that no one but her and Marcello even knew about.

"And we should not keep you from your dinner any longer," Flavia Scorsolini said.

Marcello and the others followed the now moving Giuseppe, but the former queen stopped beside Danette and put her elegant hand on her shoulder, then squeezed gently. "It was a pleasure meeting you. All of you."

Danette looked at the older woman and willed the pain inside of her to stay hidden. "Thank you," she forced out. "It was a pleasure meeting you, too."

Her companions chipped in with more of the same.

Flavia shook her head as if her thoughts troubled her. "Perhaps I will see you again."

"That is very unlikely."

Flavia cocked her head to one side and studied Danette for a nerve-racking moment. "I wonder." And then without another word, she moved on.

"Wow, that was odd. Did you think the boss was acting strangely?" Lizzy asked when Flavia was gone.

"I would say he was acting true to form," Danette replied.

"I thought I was going to die when you called him *Marcello*, and in front of his family, no less." Lizzy shivered. "I'm just glad he's not as hung up on protocol as some Italian men."

"He would never fire an employee for that kind of thing, but other men might," Ramon agreed.

Then he and Lizzy's date spent ten minutes rhapsodizing over what a great guy Marcello was and how much they admired the way he didn't trade on his royal status to run the company.

Danette let the conversation flow around her for the rest of dinner, replying only when she was asked a direct question.

Marcello's table turned out to be right in her line of sight and he had taken a seat facing her. She tried to keep her gaze from straying to him, but at one point she simply had to look and found his eyes directed at her. Their gazes locked, but she broke eye contact before he had the chance to. She'd suffered enough rejection at his hands tonight.

She was careful not to look that way again, though she felt his eyes on her more than once.

When it was time to go, Ramon offered to see her to

her door and she gratefully accepted. She had no desire to ride with Lizzy as planned earlier, not knowing then as she did now that Lizzy's boyfriend would be in the car, too. She had no desire to play fifth wheel.

Ramon stopped in front of her cottage and got out to let her out of the car. He walked her to the door and waited while she unlocked it. "Thank you for an enjoyable evening."

She didn't think she'd added much to it. It had taken all her self-control not to break down and cry. "Thank you, Ramon."

He grasped her shoulders and went to kiss her goodnight, but she pulled her head back. "I'm sorry. I don't…"

He changed the direction of his lips and kissed her cheek before stepping back and smiling. "You know, I think it is just as well. The boss kept watching you during dinner and he gave me a couple of looks that wished me to Outer Mongolia. I like my job. I think I will keep it."

"I'm sure he would never fire you for dating me."

"Perhaps not, but I do not mind not putting it to the test." Then he stood straighter. "I would date you regardless if you had offered encouragement, you understand?"

"I do understand. You're not the kind of man to be cowed." She said it for the benefit of his ego, but she thought really that she might very well be speaking the truth.

After all, he had tried to kiss her *after* deciding that Marcello was interested in her. But she hadn't encouraged him and he had decided to cut his losses.

"Watch out for him, though. He is in a league far beyond us normal mortals."

"I believe you."

She was sitting rigid in a chair by the window when Marcello arrived an hour later. She'd known he would come, but she hadn't expected him for another hour, or more. He must have cut his evening short with his family.

She wondered why. Surely he wasn't worried. His supreme male confidence would not allow him to expect anything to have changed between them from something as simple as an unexpected meeting at dinner. But it had. She couldn't stand being his secret mistress any longer.

She had the door open when he got out of his car.

He walked toward her, his expression grim. "It is a good thing Ramon is not here. The entire way over, I played one scenario after another in my head of what I would do if you were entertaining him for after dinner coffee."

"I can only imagine one scenario myself," she said quietly and without rancor. She hurt so much, there was no room for anger. "You would have turned around and driven away if you saw his car. Any other option would have risked exposing the fact that you were here to see me."

"Your imagination is sadly lacking then. My fantasies centered on a very satisfying letting of blood and definitely required me getting out of my car."

"How primitive." But she didn't believe a word of it.

"I am primitive where you are concerned."

"In bed maybe, but not out of it. Fantasies is the right word. You would never have gotten out of your car to stake a claim. Admit it."

He was inside the house now and she shut the door behind him, her movements jerky and awkward. She felt like her arms and legs did not belong to her, as if she was outside of her body looking at the carnage within and wondering at it.

"You are wrong, Danette. I *would* have gotten out of my car. Never doubt it. It is a good thing for all involved it did not come to that, but you have made your point."

"What point is that?"

"You did not like seeing the picture of me dancing with another woman. I did not like seeing you out to dinner with another man."

"You believe I went out with Ramon to teach you a lesson?"

"Yes. Why else would you go out with him?"

She could have told him for the simple reason that she'd been tricked into it, but she held her tongue. She had no desire to set his mind at ease like that. "Maybe I wanted to go out on a date with a man not ashamed to be seen with me." Maybe it was as simple as that.

"It has never been a matter of shame," he practically yelled, the false front of calm blowing sky high, just that fast.

And she realized only then that it *had* been a false front. Marcello's entire being was vibrating with dark fury.

A week ago, that would have upset her unbearably. Now she didn't even care. Let him be angry. She would be angry, too…if she didn't hurt too much. "Then why not introduce me to your family? They aren't the press and you can't tell me that they would have leaked the story, either."

"If my mother thought it would push me into marriage, do not bet yourself she would not do it."

"You don't mean that."

"You do not know her. She can be ruthless. Give her the least scent of possible romance and she will be planning the wedding and compiling the guest list, which is why I have not introduced you to my family."

"Because you never plan to marry me?"

"Because I do not want my family interfering with my private life."

She had thought she'd learned all there was to know of pain growing up with the physical deformity it had taken more than a decade to correct, but there were different kinds of pain in life. She was realizing that the pain from loving unwisely was the most intense.

But her heart, that organ which was stronger than she could ever have imagined, persisted in holding onto a tendril of hope. "You said you didn't like seeing me with Ramon."

Anger glittered in his eyes. "I did not."

"What are you going to do about it?"

"More to the point," he asked, "what are *you* going to do about it?"

"What do you mean?"

"I have admitted you made your point. There is no need for you to play the farce of dating another man again."

"That's it?" she asked incredulously, her disbelief pushing her pain aside for the moment. "You tell me you don't like something and you expect me not to do it again."

"Why not? You care about me. Our relationship is important to you. You do not wish to undermine it."

"If that is true, then shouldn't the converse be true? You know it hurt me to see that picture, but I don't see you offering to change your public image."

"But I will do so."

The tendril of hope grew stronger. "You're ready to go public with our relationship?"

"No. I told you—"

"I don't care what you told me. I can't stand it anymore, Marcello. I need our relationship to be open and honest. No more hiding."

CHAPTER SIX

"I WILL be careful not to put you in the position of seeing such a hurtful picture again."

"And will you stop behaving like you are single around other women?"

"I will not dance with them."

"That's not an answer!"

He let out an impatient breath. "I am sorry."

"Are you? Do you really care how much it hurt me to hear your brother talking about you like you don't have a relationship? Does it bother you that it rips at my heart to be dismissed by you like you did at the restaurant tonight?"

"I did not dismiss you."

"You didn't introduce me as the woman in your life, either."

"You know why."

"But the reasoning isn't enough for me anymore. I'm sorry you hate to have your private life made public, but I hate being your dirty little secret. I can't do it anymore. It hurts too much, don't you get it?" she begged, her voice cracking.

He pulled her into his arms and hugged her. "I do not wish to hurt you, *amante*. Please believe me."

The tears she'd fought all night would no longer be denied and began to flow hotly down her cheeks. "I love you, Marcello. So much. I need to know you care for me, too."

He went stiff and pulled away, his expression concerned, but no reciprocal love evident. "I do not want you to love me."

"What?"

"I told you in the beginning that our affair is temporary, that I was not looking for love and had none to give."

"We've been together six months. How do you define temporary?"

"I do not define it. We do not have a limit on our time together."

"Except that it can't be a lifetime?" she asked painfully.

"I cannot give you love and marriage."

"You can't, or you won't?"

"I loved my wife, Danette. I will never love another woman. It is the destiny of the men in my family to love only once in such a way."

She heard the words, but she could not believe them. He thought he would never love again? "Please, Marcello, I know there is always some guilt involved in falling in love again after a spouse dies, but don't throw away what we have because of it. I cannot believe Bianca would have wanted that for you."

"This is not about what Bianca would have wanted. It is about my ability to give you what you say you want."

"A public acknowledgment of my place in your life?"

"My love."

"I did not ask for that."

"You did. You love me, you said."

"I do love you."

"You want me to give you my heart as well."

"I want you to acknowledge you care for me."

"I do care."

"Enough to make our relationship public?"

"And when it ends, do you truly believe that having gone public, having made you the target of media attention is going to make that situation better for you?"

"Why does it have to end?"

He just stared at her.

She desperately searched for the right words to convince him that they had something bigger than an affair that he was determined to walk away from one day. "When we first began our relationship, you tried to keep your distance, but now we're practically living together. I'm important to your life."

She needed that to be true. Please let that be true.

"I do not deny it. We have incredible sex and I enjoy your company, but you should not be constructing castles in the sky around such things." He pulled her back into his arms, his touch gentle and comforting. "I do not wish to hurt you, but it is only fair for me to be honest. I am not looking at marriage with you."

Maybe not consciously, but she had to make him see that subconsciously she played a bigger role in his life than he gave her credit for.

"If you don't see me as part of your future then why are you so cavalier about birth control, Marcello? Half the time when we make love, you forget the condom."

If he'd gone stiff when she told him she loved him, he went positively rigid now. "That is not an indication that I see a future with you."

"What is it, then?" She leaned back to look into his face. "You aren't an irresponsible man. You wouldn't risk pregnancy if somewhere deep in your heart, you didn't think you could stand being married to me."

He grimaced, looking uncomfortable. Was she getting through to him?

"I do not risk pregnancy. Since you were a virgin and I have always practiced safe sex, I risk nothing at all."

"Don't be ridiculous. I'm not on the pill and you know it."

He sighed. "This is not something I enjoy talking about, but I see I have no choice. I am sterile, Danette. Or as good as."

"What are you talking about?" This vibrant man incapable of fathering children? She couldn't believe it.

"I was diagnosed with a very low sperm count the second year of my marriage. Bianca and I tried for children until she died, but we never conceived."

"A low sperm count is not a *no* sperm count."

"What would you know about it?"

"I spent more time in hospital waiting rooms during my childhood and teenage years than most kids spend on the playground or in the mall. I read a lot of magazines. You'd be surprised what you can pick up in *Cosmo*."

"As a child?"

"I didn't finish treatment until I was nineteen."

"What kind of treatment? Why did you never tell me about this?"

She shoved herself out of his arms. "Why didn't *you* tell *me* about your supposed sterility?"

"It was not something you needed to know."

"You're wrong. I had a right to know why you've been playing Russian roulette with my body. You assumed that if you couldn't get the woman you loved pregnant, you couldn't impregnate anyone else, either. Right?"

"It is not Russian roulette. I *cannot* get you pregnant."

"I've been such a fool. I thought you were beginning to care for me but in reality the very actions I took as proof show how very little you really do feel for me." That knowledge hurt more than anything else had tonight: how thoroughly she had duped herself into believing she mattered to him. "You think me so unimportant, so incompatible with your life that you aren't even afraid of getting me pregnant because you assume you can't. I really am nothing more than a body in your bed…an expendable secret mistress." The last words came out in a choked whisper.

"That is not true."

"The facts speak for themselves, Marcello. I only wish I'd known all of them earlier." Oh, how she wished it.

She stumbled back from him, needing more distance than her small cottage could give her. "Get out."

He put his hand out appealingly. "Danette…"

"I mean it, Marcello. Get out of my home. I don't ever want you to come here again."

"But what has changed between us? Nothing. I am the same man you received with joy into your body this afternoon."

"Again without a condom."

"I told you, pregnancy is not a risk with me."

"You're wrong, Marcello. About that and a lot of other things as well. Everything has changed. I have finally realized how little I matter to you."

"That is not true. I have already said I would change my public image."

"And you think that's some great concession?"

"It is more than I have offered another woman since my wife's death."

"How big of you."

"Damn it, *amante*—!"

"Don't call me your lover. There's no love in what you feel for me. You said so yourself."

"Do you not think I would love you if I could? I will not do to you what my father did to my mother."

"Divorce me?"

"He did not divorce her. She divorced him." He sighed. "They married because she was pregnant with me, but he had already had the love of his life and his feelings for my mother were not enough to keep him from other women. She discovered he had had an affair and she left him."

"Smart woman."

"Yes, and I am smart enough to know my own limitations."

He didn't love her. He never would. He didn't even want her enough to think he would remain faithful if they were to marry. Not that he had ever considered that kind of future with her, no matter what delusions her mind had dished up.

"I wish *I* were smart, but I was stupid enough to get involved with you and to stay in a relationship that you insisted on keeping secret because I convinced myself you cared. Ramon was right. I'm *so* not in your league, and I never will be. I was a world class idiot to think you could genuinely care for me—but then, looking at my track record, I'm not exactly Einstein where men are concerned."

"Do not compare me to that little worm you left behind in the States."

"Don't worry. You two aren't even in the same stratosphere."

"No, we are not."

"He only bruised my heart, you've decimated it. He used me to get ahead in his career, but you've just used me, period. You're leagues beyond him in the 'smarmy male who doesn't care how much he hurts a woman and uses her' stakes."

"I do care if I hurt you. Have I not said it? I was honest with you from the beginning. I risked your rejection to tell you the truth. I have been honest with you tonight, sharing a painful part of my history to show you the truth of our relationship. I am damn well not a smarmy male!"

"All that proves is that I let you use me, not that you didn't do it. But I'm not going to let you use me anymore."

"I do not use you. What we have is mutual."

"We don't have anything. Not anymore."

"That is not true, *cara*. We have something very special."

"So special you don't want anyone else to know about it. So special that not only will you never love me, but you don't want my love. That's not special, that's sex at its most basic. Worse…it's pathetic."

She could tell he was frustrated, that he didn't know what to say. She wanted to tell him, "Welcome to the club." Because she hadn't known what to say to change his mind and there was nothing he could say to change hers.

His big hands clenched into fists. "I do not want to lose you."

She shook her head, the pain of the truth crushing in its intensity. "You already have."

"I will not beg."

"I would never expect you to. What I do expect is

for you to respect me enough to leave my home when I ask you to."

He drew himself up, stiff and erect. "So be it. We can talk after you have had a chance to calm down."

"There isn't anything left to say between us."

He pulled her to him and kissed her with a tenderness that she could not combat. When he was done, she was clinging to him. "I think you are wrong. I think we still have a great deal between us."

"Sex? It isn't enough, Marcello. It never could be."

But he didn't answer. He merely put her from him gently and left.

She crumbled to the floor and sobbed her heart out as the enormity of her loss washed over her. She cried so long and so hard that she lost her voice, and the next morning she called in sick to work. He called her mid-morning and once she recognized his voice, she hung up the phone and then unplugged it. Her cell phone chirped and she turned it off, too.

She plugged the phone back in later that afternoon and called Tara. She told her everything and her friend was threatening bodily harm to Marcello ten minutes into the phone call.

"I just wish it didn't hurt so much."

"I understand, believe me, but Marcello was right about one thing…it hurts less when you don't have to share the pain and humiliation of a breakup in the public eye."

"It's a good thing we kept everything secret, then, because if it hurt any more, I think I'd die from it."

"Oh, honey." Tara sighed. "It will get better, but not right away. You just have to live one day at a time. I'm here for you if you need me. Remember that."

"I'll remember."

Marcello called again and this time she stayed on the line long enough to tell him not to call back. Amazingly he listened, and she got no more phone calls for the rest of the night. She spent those hours trying to decide if she would quit her job, or stick it out.

She couldn't imagine what running into Marcello in the office would do to her. However, in reality, except for when he contrived to see her, there was no reason for her path to cross with that of the president of the company. She'd tried running from heartache once and look where it had landed her—in far worse pain than what she'd tried to leave behind.

She went to work the next morning, still unsure what she was going to do with her future and so upset that she was nauseous with it despite the calm front she put on for her co-workers' benefit.

She was making copies of her presentation on the Cordoba project in the copy room when she felt a presence behind her.

"Good morning, *cara*."

She spun around to find Marcello standing less than a foot away. She backed up but bumped into the big machine making swishing noises as her copies spit efficiently out of its mechanism. "Marcello. What are you doing here?"

"Have we not had this conversation before?" he asked with one side of his mouth tilted in a small smile.

She sidled sideways, needing to get some distance between them. "It's highly unusual for the president of the company to find himself in the copy room."

"Not so unlikely if that is where his lover is to be found." The body she craved more than sustenance or life stood between her and freedom through the tantalizingly open doorway.

"Ex-lover," she snapped.

He stepped backward and pushed the door shut. "I am not ready for you to be my ex."

Memories of another shut door sent her heart rate into an erratic dance in her chest. She eyed the closed portal with nothing short of deep suspicion.

He smiled at her. "Do not worry. I am not planning to repeat the scene in your office…unless it becomes absolutely necessary. I simply want privacy for our discussion."

"Here is not the place."

"You threw me out of your home, hung up on me or ignored my calls altogether and have spent the morning avoiding your office. In essence, you chose this venue."

"So don't complain about it?"

"Right."

"Look, I'm sorry you aren't ready to break up, but I have no intention of waiting around for you to dump me."

He sighed with exasperation. "I do not want to dump you. Surely I have made that obvious?"

"You will, though…someday."

He shrugged, but the casual movement did not mask the ferocious tension she sensed in him. "Perhaps one day we will both decide we are better off apart, but why hasten that day if we do not have to?"

"Because I've already decided that I'm better off without you." Though her heart screamed at her that she was a liar.

"I want you to give me a chance to change your mind—"

"No," she slotted in before the seductive offer had a chance to take hold of her heart.

"This weekend at my brother's wedding celebration on Diamante," he continued as if she hadn't spoken.

"You want me to attend your brother's wedding with you?" He had to be joking. He couldn't mean it the way it sounded…like he was ready to go public with their relationship. "As what?"

"As my date."

"No way." But she said it more out of reflex than intent and her voice was weak from shock.

"You said you wanted to go public with our relationship. I am prepared to do so rather than lose you." He was rigid with tension and she knew this was hard for him.

"I didn't break it off with you in an attempt to twist your arm." She hated emotional blackmail.

"Whatever your intention, I have thought about it and realized I would rather deal with the unwanted media attention than to end our affair."

If only he had said that yesterday…before he told her he did not and would not ever love her. She would have jumped at the chance to meet his family before he made it clear how little he wanted a family with her.

"No." It was the hardest word she'd ever had to say and her wounded heart bled some more because of it.

He looked shocked, his dark complexion going pale. "What do you mean *no*?"

"Y-you were right…the p-pain of breaking up would only be increased if it…" She pause, taking a deep breath and trying to get the emotions making her stutter under control. She tried again. "If it happened in the public eye. And since there is no chance we *wouldn't* break up, you've made that clear, I don't want to set myself up for more pain and humiliation on top of it down the road."

"I do not want you humiliated. I do not want you hurt and I do not wish to break up."

"You should have thought of that before throwing my love back in my face," she said helplessly. "I don't mean to sound bitter. You told me from the beginning that you didn't love me, but I convinced myself that you cared. I deceived myself and hurt myself as much as you did."

"It was not a deception. I do care."

"Not enough."

"How can you say that? I have refused to have a liaison in the public eye since Bianca's death, but I'm willing to do so for the sake of keeping you."

"Because all it is is a liaison. I love you. I'm sorry it happened. I know it's inconvenient for you, but I can't handle being in the kind of uncommitted relationship you established anymore. It was killing me by inches and the last couple of days have hurt more than I ever want to hurt again."

"And I am doing all that I can to rectify that hurt."

"It isn't enough."

"I loved Bianca."

"I know," she said painfully, thinking she did not need the reminder.

He stalked her until she was flat against the wall and his body was less than an inch from hers. "I know what it is to hurt. And I can tell you this. If I had a chance to spend more time with Bianca, I would have taken it…no matter what the cost down the road. You say you love me. If your words were true, then you would crave the same thing."

With that, he backed up and spun on his heel and left.

She stared after him long minutes after he was gone…her mind and heart in a turmoil. How had he made her feel guilty? He was the one who spurned her love and yet he'd managed to make her feel like she didn't love him enough. And darned if his reasoning wasn't playing an insidious refrain inside of her head.

She *did* love him. Okay, so chances were that if she got back together with him, they would end up breaking up somewhere down the road. It was inevitable really because he didn't want marriage and he didn't want to love her.

But as he'd pointed out, life was uncertain. Bianca had died so young, but she wasn't unique in this world. No one knew what tomorrow might bring…no one could guarantee how many tomorrows they might have. Not her and not Marcello.

The question that preyed on her mind for the rest of that day and the next morning as she once again battled nausea was whether or not it would hurt more to continue her relationship with Marcello and risk a breakup down the road, or to force herself to go on living without him, knowing in her heart of hearts that she could have him?

He was offering her far more than a place in his bed…he was offering her a place in his life. A public place.

CHAPTER SEVEN

DANETTE battled her pain-filled thoughts and the continued on again, off again nausea as she presented her report on the Cordoba project to a room full of top sales and marketing staff.

She was halfway through the presentation and going over the PowerPoint presentation that accompanied the reports she'd handed out when someone opened the coffee carafe near her and she got a strong whiff of the aromatic beverage.

Her stomach roiled, and she slapped her hand over her mouth and sprinted for the washroom.

When her stomach finally settled, she rinsed her mouth and walked out to the lounge area of the ladies' room. The director of marketing, a chic woman in her fifties with kind brown eyes, was waiting for her.

"You should sit down for a while before trying to go back to your desk."

"The presentation…"

"I instructed Ramon to finish it for you. Your notes were clear and he'd worked on the project with you enough that he should have no trouble."

"But you're missing it."

"I'll skim through the PowerPoint slides when I go back to my desk, but I wanted to make sure you were all right. I remember feeling the same way, and you looked like it had taken you by surprise."

"You've had the flu recently, too?"

The woman laughed. "Not this kind of flu…not for more than twenty-five years."

"This kind of flu?"

"You don't know?" the director asked with a gentle smile.

But suddenly, Danette did. She hadn't had her period in six weeks, but she'd never been terribly regular, so that fact had not impinged on her consciousness. Especially not for the last few days. First she'd been missing Marcello and then she'd been fighting with him…the condition hadn't been one that left her thinking too clearly.

"It's not possible," she said, but knew it was.

"Are you sure about that?"

"He didn't think he could get me pregnant," she said, dazed and then realized what she'd said and slapped her hand over her mouth for the second time in fifteen minutes.

"And you took the risk anyway?" The director shook her head. "Young women these days…you can be so naïve."

"I wasn't being naïve." Well, maybe she had been. "Not about that. I didn't *mind* the risk."

"Here's hoping your young man feels the same way."

She doubted it. Marcello didn't want children with her. He would put a brave front on it, of that she had no doubt. No matter how angry he made her, he was still a really responsible guy, but he couldn't have made it more obvious that he didn't want a family with her if he had put it in skywriting.

She smiled weakly for the other woman's benefit. "Thank you for checking on me."

"Think nothing of it, but if I were you, I would stay away from open coffeepots."

Danette shuddered feelingly. "I intend to."

Marcello stopped in the doorway between his office and that of his assistant when he heard Danette's name.

"She ran out of the room so fast, I thought she was going to rush right into the door instead of going through it," one of the marketing people was saying.

"And the director followed her?"

"After telling Ramon di Esperanza to finish the presentation. Yes."

"I hope she's okay. Danette is a sweetheart and she's good at her job."

"Oh, I'm sure she's all right, but I don't think it's an illness that will end quickly for her, if you take my drift."

"What do you mean?" his assistant asked.

"Well, I remember being very sensitive to the scent of coffee when I was pregnant with my first child. She acted just that way. She had been fine before that."

"You think Danette is pregnant? But she's not dating anyone."

"It only takes one night."

"I don't think she is the type for a one-night stand."

The woman from marketing shrugged. "Perhaps you're right, but she is back in her office right as rain now. If that's not the pattern of morning sickness, then I don't know what is."

Marcello stumbled back into his office, his head

spinning with the ramifications of Danette being pregnant. Was the baby his?

It had to be.

But how could it be possible?

Danette's words from the night before last ran through his mind—*Low sperm count is not a no sperm count* and *Playing Russian roulette with my body.*

He had been, but he had not meant to. He could not believe he had gotten her pregnant after the years of trying with Bianca. He'd assumed he could never get a woman pregnant and had decided never to marry again because of it. He'd had enough of feeling like less than a man in his marriage with Bianca because of his inability to get her pregnant.

He'd been determined never to put himself in that situation again. His inability to plant his child in her womb had hurt them both and tainted what would have otherwise been a perfect marriage.

He could not have gotten Danette pregnant. It just wasn't possible. No. The woman from marketing had to be mistaken.

He picked up his phone.

His assistant answered, "Yes, Signor Scorsolini?"

"Please ask the director of marketing to come up to my office."

"Yes, *signor.*"

An hour later he had some answers and he was still reeling from the shock of them. Danette believed she was pregnant and she believed he was the father.

Not that she'd said so, but she'd told his marketing director that the father thought he could not get her pregnant. That meant it had to be him. Not that he could seriously doubt her fidelity.

She was his, and had been from their first date. She could not have had the pregnancy medically confirmed yet because she hadn't realized she was carrying his child until the director pointed it out. However, *he* was willing to believe.

He was desperate to believe.

The director of marketing had been hesitant at first to share the conversation she'd had in the bathroom with Danette, but being president of the company came with some privileges. Evincing concern for any one of his employees was one of them.

He'd assured the older woman he had no desire to fire Danette, merely make sure she was all right. She was a valued employee and he had hired her on the suggestion of his good friend Angelo Gordon. He was responsible for her. Which was an understatement he wasn't willing to get into. The director had understood the very Sicilian outlook.

After the woman left, a desire to celebrate fizzed through his insides as he asked his assistant to call Danette up to his office. She looked at him with a certain amount of speculation, but he let none of the emotions rioting through him show on his face. He was good at that. He'd learned early with the press hounding his every footstep not to show his feelings, not to express his vulnerability.

He'd come closer than he had in years that morning when he'd asked Danette to join him on Diamante Island for his brother's wedding. Her refusal had hurt and surprised him and it had taken the extent of his formidable control not to show how much.

After a couple of hours thinking and very little work getting done, he'd come to terms with it and even understood her point of view. She loved him, but he could make no promises for the future. However, part of him questioned how strong and real that love was if she found it so easy to walk away from him. Not that that was an option any longer.

Everything had changed and soon she would know how much.

"Miss Michaels left early today, Signor Scorsolini," his assistant said from the doorway pricking the bubble of elation surrounding him.

"I see. Do you know why?"

"I believe she was ill earlier today. She must have gone home to rest."

Marcello nodded. "Please cancel everything on my schedule through noon tomorrow."

"But Signor Scorsolini, you have—"

"Pass anything urgent on to my second in command." He had something of paramount importance to take care of and nothing else even approached it at the moment.

Danette read the pregnancy test results for something like the hundredth time and still had a hard time believing them. She carried Marcello's child. Her hand settled over her queasy stomach and she thought of the life she cradled there. She remembered reading once that morning sickness was the sign of a healthy pregnancy, and hers must be really healthy because she felt absolutely awful.

If she had the energy, she'd go looking online for suggested remedies, but she just wanted to curl up in her bed and sleep.

She was headed to do just that when a powerful pounding on her front door stopped her.

She peeked out, but didn't need her eyes to confirm what her instincts already knew. Marcello had come.

He couldn't know about the baby. Not yet. *She* barely knew about it. Maybe he'd heard she left work early for illness. Maybe he was checking on her. It wasn't such a far fetched notion. He'd always been solicitous of her health, babying her during that time of month and providing her with lots of chocolate...

Oh, man. She swallowed an urge to puke. Even the thought of chocolate was upsetting to her stomach. *Chocolate*? Who got morning sickness from chocolate? That was just wrong.

The door pounded again. "Open up, Danette. I know you're in there!"

He didn't sound solicitous so much as impatient.

She slipped the lock and opened the door. "Hello, Marcello, what brings you here."

"What do you think?" His blue gaze went over her like seeking hands.

She shrugged. "I haven't the faintest idea."

"You were sick halfway through your presentation this morning."

It shouldn't surprise her that he'd heard about it. The company grapevine was more efficient than the world's most knowing gossip columnist. "So, you were worried about me and decided to check on me?"

He pushed into the living room, gently cupping her shoulders to steady her as he moved past her. "You could say that."

"There isn't any need. I'm fine. It was just a temporary upset."

"That is not what my director of marketing called it. In fact, it was her opinion your upset would last for several months."

"Oh, no..."

He frowned at her, clearly bothered by her reaction. "Oh, yes. And I do not appreciate being the last to hear."

"Hear what?"

"That you're pregnant."

All of the air left her immediate vicinity and she swayed as everything went black around the edges. He grabbed her and then swung her up into his arms and headed to the bedroom.

"Are you all right? Have you made an appointment with the doctor?"

"I'm fine. I just got dizzy for a second. Anyway, I only just confirmed it with an at home test. I haven't had time to make, much less keep, a doctor's appointment."

"That's what the director thought, that you did not know you were pregnant."

Remembering his accusation in the other room, she stiffened in his arms. "Then what was that malarkey about you being the last to know?"

Red scored his cheekbones. "I am not thinking straight. I am sorry. Only, I wish I had heard the news from your lips first. It did not feel right the other way."

"If you ask me, nothing feels right about this situation."

He stopped in the process of laying her on the bed. "How can you say that?"

"Oh, I don't know. I'm pregnant with a child you cannot possibly want. We just broke up, and everyone's bound to think I got pregnant by a one-night stand because our relationship is top secret."

He gently settled her on the bed and then sat down beside her, his hand going possessively to her lower bell—which for some reason brought tears to her eyes.

"Naturally all that has changed. And please, do not ever say again that I do not want this baby."

"But how can you?"

"How can I not? A baby is a gift from God. A gift I thought never to have. I believed I would never be a father, now I know I will. I am not making the best of a bad situation. I am *thrilled.*" And his eyes glowed with such deep inner joy, she could not doubt him. "I want this baby more than I can ever say to you."

She'd been wrong. Dead wrong. Marcello had been absolutely convinced of his sterility. That was obvious. She'd been wrong to assume he had been careless of the consequences of unprotected sex to her: he had genuinely not believed there would be any. But that didn't mean the opposite was true…that he cared about her like she cared about him.

The man really, desperately wanted the baby in her womb, but it had nothing to do with *her* being the mother. He wanted to be a father and the fact that she was the vehicle to making that happen did not automatically give her a special place in his heart…only his life.

Reminding herself of that reality could not prevent a small smile from creasing her lips. She'd never seen Marcello so happy and she liked it.

"I'm glad you're pleased about the baby."

"I am that, *tesoro mio,* supremely pleased." He grinned at her and rubbed a slow circle on her lower tummy. "I wonder if we can arrange a double wedding with my brother? He planned to keep it very low-key and it would be perfect."

"What in the world are you talking about?"

"We must marry as soon as possible."

Well, she hadn't been wrong about *that* anyway. He wanted to marry her, as she'd been sure he would if he ever got her pregnant, but the prospect did not hold nearly the appeal it once had for her, when she'd believed he cared about her. But she wasn't going to dismiss it out of hand, either.

Her reaction to the prospect of attending his brother's wedding had been enough to convince her that no matter what feelings Marcello did or did not have, for her, she loved him. Walking away from him was a path paved with pain.

"You're going too fast for me, Marcello."

"What do you mean? You cannot tell me that you don't want to marry me." His joyful acceptance of impending fatherhood gave way to ruthless resolve. "According to you, the greatest drawback to continuing a relationship with me was the prospect it would one day end. Once we are married that bogeyman is laid to rest permanently."

"It wasn't a bogeyman."

"Whatever. The fear will be groundless in marriage."

"Marriages end all the time…in divorce." He knew that better than most. Look at his own parents.

The possessive hand on her tummy was joined by one on her shoulder, as if he was holding her so she would not run away. "There will be no divorce."

"There will be if you think you're going to get away with being unfaithful like your father was." Memories of what he'd told her about his parents' marriage plagued her. "I'm no more tolerant of that sort of thing than your mother was."

He drew himself up and jumped to his feet, towering beside the bed like an enraged avenging angel. "How do you dare accuse me of such a thing? I have never been unfaithful in this relationship and I consider marriage vows sacrosanct."

"You're the one that told me you weren't planning to remarry because you didn't trust yourself to be faithful."

"That was before."

"Before what?"

"You are pregnant with my child," he said, as if that should explain everything.

"Well, your mother had your father's child, too, and that didn't stop him."

He crossed his arms and glared at her. "I am not my father. I won't behave like him."

"How can you be sure?" For that matter, how could she?

"Because I am, all right? I give you my word that I will never take another woman to my bed."

"I'm sure your father gave his word, too."

"Are you refusing to marry me?" Marcello asked, his voice laced with furious disbelief. "Think carefully before you answer because I warn you, married or not, I will not play the role of part-time father in my child's life."

Oh, man. She didn't even want to know what he was implying here. "I wouldn't want you to and I'm not refusing to marry you. I'm only saying I need time to think. This morning I was not in a relationship with you any longer—"

"By your choice, not mine."

"Yes, agreed, but if you can't see that what led up to our break-up is a cause for concern for me, I don't know what to say to help you see it. And frankly, it's thrown me for a complete loop to discover I'm pregnant."

"A good loop, I trust."

She turned her head away, old fears surfacing to plague her. How could she answer that? In most ways, she was totally thrilled to be pregnant with his child, but she couldn't forget the doubts that had led her to making the choice never to have children. She hadn't vanquished them nearly as much as she'd believed she had.

"You do not want my child?" he asked, sounding ten times angrier than he had been before.

She shook her head, but still didn't want to look at him. She couldn't think straight when she was looking at him and right now she needed to think. "It's not that."

"What is it then?"

"I hadn't planned to get pregnant."

"Now, or ever?"

"Ever."

"You did not do anything to prevent it, even though I often forgot the contraception."

"I know." Because she'd hoped and dreamed…only sometimes when dreams came true they could be terrifying.

"So, you had to have thought of pregnancy a little?"

"I did, but it was more fantasy than reality."

"And now that it is reality, you are unhappy?"

"Not unhappy…frightened," she admitted.

His weight came down on the bed beside her again and his hand touched her temple in a gentle caress. "Why frightened? Because of your career?"

"Because of my genes."

"What does what you wear have to do with having a child?"

She gave a choked laugh. "Not those kind of jeans." He deserved the truth. He had a right to know what kind of risks their child faced, but she had to scramble inside her mind for the right words. This was not a conversation, she had ever planned to have. "There's something I need to tell you, Marcello."

"You are not already married. You were a virgin the first time we made love—of course you could not be married," he said as if speaking to himself.

She turned back to face him and smiled, albeit weakly. "No. I am not already married."

"And the baby is mine. Do not try to convince me otherwise because it will not wash. You are a one-man woman and I am your man."

"Of course the baby is yours, and I have no intention of trying to convince you otherwise."

"Then nothing else could be bad enough to justify your look of unhappiness."

"That's what you think."

"So, then tell me whatever troubles you and I will fix it."

"You can't."

"You are so sure about this?" he asked as he took her hand in his and rubbed his thumb against her palm.

"Yes. In this case, there is nothing either of us can do but wait and hope."

"Tell me."

"I'm sorry." She swallowed. "I don't mean to make such a meal of it. It's just really hard for me to talk about, but I'd decided when I was fifteen, I think it was, that I would never have children."

"And why is that?" he asked with an indulgent look.

"Because I'd spent the last nine years of my life in a full torso brace to correct a genetic spinal deformity, and I knew I had more years to go, and I hated the thought of putting my own child through the same thing."

"*Che cosa?*"

"When I was six years old, I was diagnosed with a severe case of idiomatic juvenile scoliosis. It's an extremely rare form of the disease; the only form more rare is that found in an infant. My doctors hoped to avoid the major surgery required to correct the disease."

"I did not know that scoliosis required surgical treatment."

"It doesn't always, but in rare cases the risk of death from stress to the heart by the deformed rib cage or paralysis are so high that the only slightly less risky surgery is suggested. My parents and my doctors wanted to avoid that, but in order to do so, I had to wear a brace pretty much twenty-four seven until I was nineteen years old and the doctors were convinced that I had stopped growing. Even so, for two years after that, I was terrified my spine would revert to the curvature that is so disabling."

"You say this disease is hereditary?"

"No, not exactly, but my mother had it and so did I. What if our baby is born with it, too? I'm sorry. I should have told you about it sooner, but I'd convinced myself that if I did conceive that it would be meant to be and that our baby would not suffer my childhood. Only now that I'm pregnant, it's all I can think about. I'm so scared, Marcello."

He pulled her into his arms, wrapping her in his embrace. "You are fine now? There is no risk to your health with this pregnancy?"

"No. None. I had an eighty percent curvature correction. It was a miracle, really, and there are no limitations on my lifestyle left over from the scoliosis."

"So your fears are all for our child?"

She nodded against his shirtfront. "I'm sorry," she said again, her voice choked with tears.

"Stop apologizing. This baby is a gift. Believe it."

She looked up at him and the warmth in his eyes filled her with hope. "But…"

"Look at you. You are well now. Even if our children were to have this disease, it does not have to be life-altering."

She grimaced with remembered pain. "Tell that to a thirteen-year-old girl who looks in the mirror and sees only the brace, not the body beneath it."

"The brace is very unwieldy?"

"No. In fact, with the right clothes, you could barely tell I was wearing it, but my parents…especially my mother…were very protective of me. They never forgot I had it on and neither did I."

"In what way were they protective?"

"Mom encouraged me to avoid physical contact with others so they wouldn't know about my brace and I wouldn't have to try to explain it."

"And did they hug you?"

"No. I didn't encourage physical touch with *anyone*."

"That explains much."

"What do you mean?"

"Nothing important. It is only that sometimes you have an invisible wall around you."

"I never noticed that stopping you from touching me."

"It did not, and it would not stop me touching our child."

Tears spilled over her eyelids at that assurance. "I'm glad, but that isn't the only thing you have to take into account."

"What else?"

"Interaction with other children. Both my parents were concerned about me playing with other children and I spent grade school recesses inside, reading and doing schoolwork, rather than playing with other children."

"How did you get your exercise?"

"My parents had me on a very specific regime, one with no chance of me being tackled by another child, or hurt in any way."

"Was that necessary?" he asked, looking dubious.

"Actually not, but that isn't the point is it? The point is that—"

"Our child will be ours and we will do our best for her regardless of what challenges she might face in life."

"It isn't that simple."

"Yes, Danette, it is."

"Don't you think my parents did their best by me?"

"Yes, but they are not us, any more than I am my father. We will be different parents."

"But you are so worried about the press. Can you imagine what they would do if they got wind of something like that?"

"If our child were to have the disease, we would go public with it and detooth the tiger before he had a chance to strike. Understood?"

"Yes. I am sorry I didn't warn you, Marcello."

"I told you to stop saying you are sorry. All right? If you truly believe that what you have told me has impacted my joy at prospective fatherhood, or the way that I will feel about our child, then you do not know me as well as I believed that you did."

"We established that the day before yesterday when

I realized all the assumptions I'd made about you had been faulty. Now I realize the other assumptions I made were equally faulty. The truth is, I'm pretty confused about you right now and learning I'm pregnant with your baby hasn't improved that any."

CHAPTER EIGHT

HE GRIMACED. "As long as we are handing out apologies, I am sorry that I hurt you."

She winced tiredly. "I really don't want to talk about it right now." She yawned. "It's not that I don't want to talk at all, but I'm just so sleepy…I'm too tired to work anything out in my head, much less discuss it. Do you mind?"

"No. Whatever you might like to think, we have a whole lifetime to work out our differences. But I am not going to pretend I did not ask you to marry me."

"But you didn't."

"What?" he demanded in a dangerously soft voice.

"You didn't *ask*. You told me that for the sake of our unborn baby we should marry."

For the second time in as many days, red scorched the skin along his sculpted cheekbones. "I should have asked, but I got carried away with my delight."

It was such an endearing admission, she patted his chest in approval. "No matter what happens, I'm really, really glad you're happy about the baby."

"Only one thing is going to happen. We are going to marry."

"I'll think about it. That's the best I can do, right now. I mean it. My mind is in a muddle and I feel like I have the flu, and I'm so tired, I could fall asleep standing up."

"Then it is a good thing you are lying down. I will look into an effective remedy for your morning sickness, but for now I will get you some crackers and weak tea. My marketing director said that was something that used to help her."

He carefully laid her back against the pillows and then got up to leave.

He came back a few minutes later and cajoled her into eating half a dozen saltines and drinking a glass of water. Afterward, she slipped into sleep, secure in the fact that Marcello was watching over her and their baby.

When she awoke two hours later, Marcello's warmth surrounded her. It felt so good that she didn't move, not wanting the sensation of peace and safety to end.

"You are awake?" he asked from behind her.

"Yes, how did you know?"

"Your breathing pattern changed."

"Oh."

"My mother has invited us to have dinner with her tonight."

She went stiff with shock. "Your mother?"

What had he been doing while she was sleeping, calling newspapers and making announcements?

He turned her to face him. "My mother. She is ecstatic about the baby, but equally thrilled I am finally remarrying."

"You told her about the baby? You told her that we were getting *married*?" Every trace of lingering sleepiness vanished in the face of his revelations.

"We are close. She would be hurt if I did not tell her."

"But I never said I would marry you!"

"You will."

Danette took a deep breath and let it out slowly. "You are so darn arrogant."

"It runs in the family."

"No doubt."

"So, you will come to dinner and make my mother happy?"

"I don't know if I'll make her happy or not, but I would like to get to know her." She only wished it had happened before she got pregnant, that Marcello had wanted the meeting for her sake and not only that of their child.

"Did I not say that we would probably see one another again?" Flavia Scorsolini asked after kissing Danette's cheeks in greeting in the huge entry hall of the Sicilian villa.

"You said that?" Marcello asked. "When?"

"You had left for our table already. The looks you were giving the girl and the man with her at the restaurant that night…they spoke very eloquently to one who knows you as well as I do. But I did wonder what my son's girlfriend was doing at a restaurant with another man." She smiled at Danette. "It all became clear when Marcello explained the reason for not yet introducing us, though you had been together for six long months."

"It did?" Danette asked.

"Yes. He kept you a secret, and any man foolish enough to play that kind of game with his woman deserves to see her out with another man on occasion, though I trust it would only have taken one time for him to mend his ways."

Marcello laughed. "As always, you are too wise,

Mama. I had promised never to be caught dancing with another woman already."

"Ah, the pictures." Flavia gave Danette a sad smile. "Seeing them must have hurt a great deal."

"Yes."

"I am surprised you agreed to marry Marcello afterward."

He sucked in a tight breath. "Mama…" he said warningly.

But Danette smiled. "I haven't. Not yet. I promised to think about it."

"For the sake of the baby?" the older woman pressed as she led them into the sitting room.

Danette sat in the red velvet armchair Flavia indicated, before taking a matching one opposite the small table. Marcello sat down on the end of the long white sofa nearest Danette.

The startling red-and-white color combination with gold accents in the sitting room was very impacting and Danette said so.

"Thank you. I designed it myself. A hobby of mine," Flavia admitted. "Now, tell me…do you plan to marry my son for the sake of the baby?"

The look that Flavia gave her was so vulnerable that Danette had no desire to prevaricate in any way. Whatever Marcello's feelings for her, she would not pretend hers were other than what they were.

"If I marry Marcello, it will also be for my sake. I love your son."

Flavia nodded as if pleased. "Yes. I can see that you do. The way you looked at him the other night was very telling as well…or should I say, the way you avoided looking at him?"

"You must be a very adept people-watcher. My friends at the table had no idea anything was up between Marcello and me."

"None at all?"

"Well, my date, Ramon, noticed that Marcello kept looking at me. He thought Marcello might be interested in me and he warned me off of him."

"Smart man. Marcello is a dear son, but his reputation as a playboy…*ai, ai, ai.*"

"Mama!" Marcello protested.

"As if your young woman did not know?" She rolled her eyes. "Danette strikes me as an astute young lady. Too smart not to realize what a bad risk you are. She's shown tremendous courage in falling in love with you."

Danette didn't know whether to laugh, or to cry. The former queen had zero tact where her son was concerned, but Danette had the distinct impression it was on purpose.

"I loved his father, you know," Flavia said to Danette. "Love is no deterrent to pain. I should know."

Marcello paled, his blue gaze filling with real anger. "Mama, she has enough reservations about marrying me. She does not need you adding to them."

"Good. I went into marriage with your father blind and lived to regret it, but she will not be so foolish."

"Do you think Marcello would have an affair?" Danette asked with an honest need to know.

Marcello cursed angrily under his breath, but Flavia's militant stance relaxed and she smiled with warm affection at her son before turning her gaze back to Danette. "No. I do not. If you want to know the truth, I think that if I had stayed married to his father, he would not have strayed again, either. He was still feeling guilty for sleeping with me so soon after the death of his beloved first wife. His behavior was entirely self-destructive."

"If you believed that, why did you leave him?" Marcello asked in a driven tone.

"I did *not* believe it at first. I was hurting desperately. It took me several years to realize that he was driven by guilt and a need to punish himself for his supposed crime. I believe that in the same way, he has spent over twenty years punishing himself for the crime of infidelity to me."

Marcello looked quite stunned. "But…"

"I know he gave you boys that song and dance about Scorsolini men only loving once, but really, can you not see how he has protected his heart all these years by never letting another woman get as close as his first wife and I did?"

"I wonder if you are right."

"You yourself said I am a wise woman, but I am worried about him. If he does not stop the self-punishment, he is going to go into his old age a lonely man."

Personally Danette could never see King Vincente as lonely, but she wondered if Flavia was right.

"If you believe all this, why in the world are you trying to talk Danette out of marrying me?" Marcello asked with angry exasperation.

"Because she must count the cost. You, too, have decided to protect your heart and refuse to love her."

"How can you know that?" Marcello demanded belligerently.

"Because if you had told her you loved her, she would have agreed to marry you already. Is that not true?"

Danette nodded. "If he meant it, yes."

"You see?"

"Mama, I love you dearly, but this is not something I wish to discuss with you, or in front of you."

"No doubt. It is embarrassing to parade your mistakes in front of your beloved mother, is it not?"

"Whether Danette and I marry is strictly between us."

"If you believe that, then you shouldn't have told your mother that it was a done deal," Danette said, humor at the situation making her lips twitch.

Marcello made the sound of a frustrated lion at bay. "Shall we go into dinner?" he asked from between clenched teeth.

Flavia smiled a knowing smile. "By all means, my son. Let us eat. It is not good to make a pregnant woman wait."

Danette didn't know how it happened, but the subject of her scoliosis came up over dinner and Flavia asked numerous questions. "So, really, there is no reason to believe your children would be so afflicted at all, is there?"

"But my mother had it and then I had it…"

"And you were both diagnosed as *idiomatic* which implies that there is no known reason for the condition. Genetics would be a *known* reason, yes?"

"Yes."

"Then you are worrying for nothing. If your children were to be similarly afflicted, then you would deal with it the same as you would deal with any issue. Your love for them would cover everything you do—and of course, you would have my expert advice for help."

Danette burst out laughing as did Marcello.

"When you told me arrogance ran in your family, I

assumed you meant from your father's side, but I see now that you got a double dose. No wonder you have the bearing of the oldest son and heir to the throne."

Flavia shook her head, humor gleaming in her dark eyes. "Marcello would hate to be king…the role is much too much in the public eye."

"This is true," Marcello said dismissively. "Besides which, Claudio is forced to endure matters of state that would bore me to death."

"But there is no denying my son did inherit more than his share of masculine confidence and a certain amount of family arrogance," Flavia said with a small laugh.

Marcello just shrugged.

"So, you will be coming to Tomasso and Maggie's wedding, will you not?" Flavia asked.

"I invited her," Marcello said.

"Your most recent invitation was given in the guise of a suggestion we make it a double wedding, if I recall correctly." And Danette would be the first to admit that her thoughts from earlier were still a little muddled.

"*Idiota*," his mother said affectionately. "If Danette agrees to marry you, there will be no hole-in-the-corner affair to raise eyebrows and prod the paparazzi into speculation. We will have a proper Sicilian wedding."

"Have you forgotten she is pregnant?" Marcello demanded. "I would prefer to have the deed done before our child makes its advent into the world."

His mother simply shook her head. "With your money and your family's influence, you can have a wedding with all the trimmings in a month's time, though that is pushing the bounds of propriety where invitations to the event are concerned."

"I do not care who comes to the wedding," he growled.

"I do," Danette said. "My mom would be devastated if she couldn't invite all of her friends and our family to my wedding. If I agree to marry you, you'll have to be okay with that."

Marcello's blue gaze burned with impatience. "So what you are saying to me is that if you finally deign to marry me, I will have to content myself with a big, Sicilian wedding that could take months to organize?"

"I did not say that. Like your mom pointed out, when you're as rich as Croesus and royal in the bargain, you can get a lot done in a short amount of time."

"So, you are saying you will marry me?"

"I didn't say that," she replied with a fair amount of her own impatience. "Stop trying to bulldoze me. It won't work."

"I told you that I loved Vincente when I married him," Flavia said.

Thankful for the change in conversation, Danette smiled gratefully. "Yes."

"Had I not been pregnant, I would not have agreed to marriage, because I knew the risk was great that he would not let himself love me. Ever."

"So you married for my sake," Marcello said.

Flavia sighed, her memories not all pleasant by the look in her lovely brown eyes. "Yes. It is hard enough to be born of royal blood in today's world full of vultures and the paparazzi without being born illegitimate. I paid a price for my folly, but I cannot say that I regret that price. For had I not paid it, you would have until the day you died."

Danette got the point and her heart contracted at the

thought of her child being hurt by a decision she made. "I see what you are getting at."

Flavia smiled, oh so gently. "I knew you would, but still you must make up your own mind. Only keep the thought that life for royalty is not like life for everyone else. You can be dirt-poor and have nothing in your life of interest in the way of accomplishments and still be the target of media attention simply because you carry a title with your name."

After that, Flavia made a determined effort to keep the conversation on less volatile topics and Danette enthusiastically aided her in that endeavor.

Marcello downshifted the powerful Ferrari and took the turn with neat precision. He and Danette had left his mother's villa five minutes before. He did not know what mood she was in; he'd learned in the last few days to take nothing for granted. That included what he would term peaceful silence coming from the other side of the car.

"You enjoyed meeting my mother," he fished, wanting to know what she was thinking.

Danette shifted perceptibly in her seat, as if she'd only now remembered he was there.

His muscles tensed. He was unused to not being the center of her thoughts when they were together. He did not like it.

"What?" she asked, clearly struggling to remember what he'd said. "Oh, yes. I like her very much. Wasn't that wild, what she said about your dad?"

"It actually makes a strange kind of sense."

"Yes, but it sure blows holes in the Scorsolini men only ever loving once theory, doesn't it?"

"Does it? Mama did not say she believed Papa loved her, only that he was punishing himself for betraying her." But his father's love life, or lack thereof, was not what interested Marcello at the moment.

"Mama made a good point about giving our child legitimacy for the sake of its future."

"Yes, she did."

"So, now will you consent to marry me?"

"Are you saying that a paper marriage for the sake of our child legally holding your name is all that you want?"

Where did she get her ideas? "No. I want you to be my wife, not merely a wife on paper."

"You didn't want that yesterday."

"Today is different."

"Yes, today, you have discovered that you are going to be a father. That's got to be very emotional for you." She said it musingly, like she was trying to work something out in her head.

"Considering the fact I thought I would never father a child, yes." He did not want to dwell on those feelings however. They were best forgotten. "I should have introduced you to my mother earlier."

"That would have undermined the secrecy of our association. You heard her. She knew there was something up between us when she met me in the restaurant and you were pretending you didn't know me. If you had introduced us before that and tried to pass me off as a mere employee, it wouldn't have been any more successful."

"I did not mean that. I meant I should have introduced you as my girlfriend to her earlier."

Danette didn't reply, her attention fixed on the darkness beyond the window.

"And I did not pretend I did not know you the other night," he said for good measure.

"It felt like it."

"I treated you the same as I treated everyone else at the table." Which he could now see had been a monumental mistake.

Because she'd taken that to mean she wasn't special to him and she was. He wanted her in a way he wanted no one else.

She looked at him. "It hurt, because I *wasn't* everyone else."

"I did not mean to hurt you. You must know this."

"Part of me does know it, but the hurting part doesn't care much what your intentions were."

How was he supposed to answer that? He could not fix it, which was his natural inclination. All he could do was try once again to explain. "I did not know you had grown completely intolerant of the need to protect our relationship with discretion. When we discussed it the night I came home from Isole dei Re, I thought you were angry about the picture in the tabloid, not the secrecy surrounding our time together."

"The picture destroyed my sense of peace about our relationship."

"For which I have apologized."

"But it could not have been taken if our relationship had not been a secret."

"You have a point, but even you must admit that in the beginning, you got quite a charge out of that secrecy. How was I to know your reaction to it had changed so drastically?"

Surely she had to see that.

"It *was* romantic in the beginning." She sighed. "We

were sneaking around and that added the seductive element of the forbidden to our intimacy. Yet we weren't doing anything wrong. Not really."

"Not at all."

"I'm pregnant and we're not married. Trust me, my mom would say we'd done something wrong. There's a reason why sex outside of marriage is a bad idea."

"I am not ashamed that you are pregnant by me."

"I know. You're actually pretty proud of the fact."

An unfamiliar sense of embarrassment assailed him. He *was* proud in a wholly uncool way that he'd managed to plant his seed in her body. "Are you ashamed to be pregnant with my child?"

"I can't be blasé about being a single pregnant woman, I'm not that sophisticated. But no, I'm not ashamed."

"You do not have to be single and pregnant. You could be married and pregnant. You could be a princess. Does that carry no weight with you?"

"I think every little girl dreams of growing up and becoming a princess, but I'm not a little girl anymore. For me, marriage has to be about a whole lot more than living out a fairy tale."

"But it is about more. You carry my child in your body."

She sighed again. He was starting to hate that sound.

"Are we back to the paper marriage for the sake of the baby then?"

"I told you, I do not want a paper marriage. I want a real marriage."

"I don't like feeling like I'm the extra baggage that comes along with the baby."

He zoomed through a yellow light, pressing the accelerator just slightly. "I don't see you that way."

"It feels like it."

"I did not want to break up before I knew you were pregnant." Surely that should count for something. "And I invited you to my brother's wedding before that as well."

"You like sex with me. I've always known it."

Anger coursed through him. She was determined to see things in the most unflattering light possible. "And *you* like sex with *me*, but you do not see me accusing you of wanting me only because of it, or for the wealth I can give you."

"Why in the world would you?"

"Because most women in my life have wanted me for my title and my money…it would be all too easy to put you in the same camp."

"Do you?"

"No."

"Then the comparison isn't valid."

"It is. You accuse me of wanting you for sex and the baby you carry, but I have never once said that was all I wanted from you. Nor has our relationship in the past exhibited such a thing."

"You kept me a secret."

"Because I hate the intrusiveness of the paparazzi in my life, not because I was ashamed of you, or did not value you. In the beginning you understood this and while I comprehend how the photo hurt you, I don't think you can dismiss the fact that up until very recently, you were perfectly content with our status quo. Holding me accountable for a change of heart I did not know about is unreasonable."

She had to see that. She was a smart, logical woman and she had always been fair-minded in the past.

"But you didn't just keep me a secret from the press.

You didn't tell your family about me, because you *didn't want to marry me.* How can you say that your sudden volte-face regarding marriage isn't the result of my pregnancy? Of course it is, and that makes me the extra baggage that comes along with a baby, not a woman desired for her own sake."

"No, it does not. I do want you for your own sake. Your pregnancy has precipitated my proposal happening *now,* but I would have gotten around to introducing you to my family and sought marriage eventually regardless." It had taken a lot of thinking after she kicked him out of her house, but he'd ultimately reached that conclusion.

Not that he would have admitted it to her. He had still been fighting the eventual outcome, but he wasn't fighting it anymore.

CHAPTER NINE

SHE gasped, her attention firmly welded to him. "Now, you are rewriting history. Don't say stuff like that. It isn't fair."

"I am not rewriting history. I want you in my life. To keep you, I was willing to go public with our relationship. You are an addiction I cannot break, one I have no *desire* to give up. If the alternative was losing you, I would have married you. I am sure of it."

"Do you hear what you're *saying*?" She sounded very upset and she was practically shouting.

He didn't know what had bothered her so much about what he had said, but it was not good for her to get so worked up in her condition. "Calm down, *amante*."

"Don't tell me to calm down! You just got through saying that if I'd blackmailed you into marriage by withholding my body, it would have worked. Even in your arrogant brain, that can't be seen as a compliment."

"It certainly was not an insult and I did not use the word blackmail."

"But that's exactly what you were talking about. Emotional blackmail—and it is something I abhor."

"Why so adamant?"

"My mother excelled at it. My parents were overprotective and there were times I rebelled…like the year I joined a soccer team in grade school. My doctors said it should be fine, but Mom was scared I'd be hurt. She pulled out the guilt guns to get me to drop the team. It was always about how much she and my dad sacrificed for me, how much she would worry and how unfair that would be to her. Never mind that her fears strangled my childhood."

"You would not do that to our child."

"No, I wouldn't, but I wouldn't do it to you, either."

"I did not say that you would."

"You implied it."

"No, I did not." Were all pregnant women so irrational? "I said that, given the choice between watching you walk out of my life and marriage, I would have married you."

"Gee, thanks. A begrudging marriage is every girl's dream for life."

He grimaced at her sarcasm. "I can say nothing right with you, can I?" he asked in a driven tone.

"I'm sorry. It's just that I'm having a hard time believing you."

"That is obvious."

"Before, you said marriage was never on the cards, and now you say that it would have been even without a baby. Don't you think that's a little inconsistent?"

"I also said I would *never* go public with a private relationship, but I was prepared to do it for you. Listen, *cara*," he said through teeth gritted with the frustration of trying to explain something she was determined not to get, "I know you did not break up with me with the intention of forcing my hand."

He reached over and squeezed her thigh and then left his hand on her leg, needing the physical connection. "Had you done so, you would not be the woman you are, and therefore such a compelling addiction for me. Most likely, in that scenario, it would not have worked, but the net result was the same. If the way I have expressed myself is clumsy, I am sorry. I only meant to say that marriage was no more a certain dead loss between us than me claiming you as my lover in a public way."

"I don't know what to believe."

"We have established that. But I do not lie to you. I never have," he said, his own temper fraying around the edges.

"You can't know you would have wanted to marry me if I wasn't pregnant. You're only guessing at that... saying it because you think it's what I need to hear."

"And do you need to hear it?"

"No. Yes... I don't know!"

"If it is not, what *do* you need to hear, *tesoro*? Tell me what the big obstacle is in your mind to our marriage."

She laughed, but it was not a humor-filled sound. "I need to know you love me."

"Like you love me?" he asked, his anger growing.

Words were all that held her back? A simple declaration of love to match her own?

"Yes," she said defiantly.

He took his hand from her thigh, fury that he did not understand roiling through him. "You were willing to walk away from me, to cut me completely from your life. As far as I know, you still are. You refuse to marry me, even for the sake of our unborn child. *That* is the kind of love you want me to feel for you?"

"I—"

"You want me. You enjoy my company. But love? I doubt it. Love is not that easily dismissed."

"I didn't dismiss you."

"What would you call your refusal to get back together, to accept the olive branch I offered to keep you in my life?"

"I do love you."

"They are just words, Danette, and they mean nothing in the face of actions that prove otherwise. But if saying them will make you more amenable to marriage…then I love you. Now, will you marry me?"

"No!"

"Why not? I've given you the words you said you wanted."

"There has to be feeling behind them."

"Like your so-called feelings for me?" he asked scathingly. "Trust me, there is more than enough feeling behind them. The feeling of wanting to go into the future with you at my side."

"Stop it! You're twisting everything I'm saying."

"Perhaps I learned that skill from you."

"Please, Marcello. I don't want to argue anymore."

He pulled into the driveway of her small cottage, stopping close to the front steps, his movements jerky. Anger pulsed through him, but he knew he had to get it under control. "I'm coming inside."

"Not to argue more," she said pleadingly and with an expression that would have moved a rock to compassion.

Even a very angry Sicilian rock.

"I do not want to argue with you."

Her eyes filled with tears. "I don't want to argue with you, either."

"Then let us go inside, *cara*."

* * *

Hours later, he held Danette curled close into his body, but he was nowhere near sleep. How was he going to convince her to marry him…and soon? He did not want her to walk down the aisle on the verge of giving birth.

He'd thought for sure that his mom's lecture on the pains of being royal and illegitimate would carry enough weight to sway her. She was a compassionate woman after all, but she had still refused to commit to the marriage.

She said she wanted love, but he had to acknowledge that saying the words in the way he had done in the car wasn't going to help his case. He wasn't sure he could give them to her otherwise, though. He had loved Bianca, and the feelings he had for Danette were entirely different.

Other than their inability to have children, his life with Bianca had been near perfect. They'd been friends since childhood and hardly ever fought. Things hadn't been perfect, and he would always carry that burden of guilt. However, he knew he had loved her and Bianca had loved him, though, like Danette, that love had had limits he had not recognized until too late.

Even before the debacle of the photo spread on his father's party, his relationship with Danette had been more volatile. She challenged him in ways his Sicilian wife never had.

And their sexual relationship was very different than what he'd known with Bianca, too. He wanted Danette with a consuming passion that broke through his control in a way his desire for Bianca had never done. He wouldn't have had sex with her on a desk under any circumstances. For him, *obsession* best described his feelings for Danette, but she wanted the hearts and flowers.

He'd prefer the actions that backed up the sentiments. If she loved him, she would agree to marry him…she would not have walked away from him without a backward glance. No, he had to think her real hang-up was because he had denied wanting to marry her before she'd gotten pregnant. Her feminine pride was smarting and he couldn't fix it.

He couldn't alter the past. Not even a prince had that power. He had tried to tell her that he would have wanted to marry her eventually anyway, that his saying the contrary was only so much hot air when weighed against losing her. That had offended her, too.

But the truth was, only his knowledge of his supposed sterility had held him back before. He hadn't realized it, hadn't wanted to face the unpalatable truth. What man wanted to acknowledge such a deficiency? Certainly no prince of the Scorsolini family.

Because of that, he'd convinced himself and her that he had balked at a long-term commitment because he had been unsure of his ability to be faithful. However, lying there in the dark next to a body he knew he would crave until the day he died, he had no choice but to admit the truth.

He, Marcello Scorsolini, Prince of Isole dei Re, had hidden like a craven boy behind that excuse rather than face being less of a man than he wanted to be. He hadn't wanted to go through the demoralizing attempts at trying to make a baby and failing as he had in his marriage to Bianca. He had not wanted to ever face losing another woman the way he had lost her. But cowardice was its own punishment and he had played the coward. Now he faced the punishment—a lack of trust from his woman that should not be there.

He had wanted to protect Danette, too. It hadn't all

been about him. He had not wanted to put another woman through the pain his sterility had brought to Bianca. Only one thing had hurt more than knowing he was a failure as a man in that department: knowing that his inability to give Bianca a baby had become a festering wound in her heart.

And in the end, it had killed her. In denying himself a future with Danette, he had also been protecting her.

She wouldn't see it that way, though. She could have no idea what it did to a woman to crave children and not be able to have them. She was standing safely on the other side of an abyss that had haunted him for close to a decade and Bianca for every year of their short marriage. Danette would never feel the dark cold that wafted up from its depths to chill a man or woman's soul.

And he was glad of that, but because she was innocent of that kind of pain, she could not comprehend what a miracle her pregnancy was. Nor could she give full credence to how very much their child deserved everything they could give…including a stable and settled home life with married parents.

She was too busy being offended he hadn't wanted to marry her before, and trying to decide if he was a good risk or not.

She'd believed him when he said he was uncertain of his faithfulness factor. She wasn't about to dismiss that issue now, even if he was ready to.

He was not proud of his stupidity in hiding behind that excuse, but once again, he had no power to alter the past.

However, that did not mean he would give up. He *would* convince her to marry him. Other than his inability to get Bianca pregnant, he was not a man who failed. He had doubled Scorsolini Shipping's income in Italy through tenacity and his ability to fix problems and find solutions.

Danette would not know what hit her if she thought she was walking out of his life with his child in her womb.

He wasn't walking away from her, either. From this point on, they would be together, married or not. If she refused to move into his home, then he would move in with her. And he would sleep on the bloody sofa if she denied him her bed. He was in it now because she'd fallen asleep before she could tell him not to share it, though he had no doubt that in the mood she'd been in…had she been awake when he came to bed, she would have.

She would probably call his actions sneaky. He called them desperate.

Marcello took Danette to the doctor's office the next morning to confirm her pregnancy. He asked loads of pertinent questions, but for every one he asked, Danette had two.

The one area of medicine she had avoided reading about while she hung out in doctor's waiting rooms as a teenager was pregnancy. It had hurt too much to read about something she planned to deny herself, but now she wanted to know *everything*.

The doctor was really forthcoming, but Marcello still thought they should stop at a bookstore and get some printed material on it. They walked out of the store an hour later with two shopping bags full of books and magazines on pregnancy, parenting and early childhood development.

"You aren't seriously going to read all of those books, are you?" she demanded as he tucked her into the back of the limousine with as much care as if she were made of Dresden china.

He'd been seriously nice to her all morning despite their ugly argument in the car the night before and the fact that she'd been less than pleasant when she woke up beside him that morning. He didn't argue with her. He didn't bring up marriage. He simply took care of her and it felt very, very strange and very, very good.

"*Sì*." He smiled indulgently at her as he slid into the seat beside her. "And do not try to tell me that you will not read them all, too. You picked half of them out."

"Yes, but somehow I just don't think we need advice on what to do for a color-blind child." She'd laughed out loud when she'd seen the clerk ring that title up, but it was only marginally more comical than him buying the book on how to teach an infant to swim. "The baby isn't even born yet! Besides, there's no reason to believe she'll be color-blind."

"Or that he won't be. You can't be too prepared."

Danette laughed. "You are a real case, you know that?"

"I am going to be a father. I think I'm entitled."

"You're so proud of yourself for knocking me up that I'm surprised your head fit through the car door."

"And yet, it did fit," he said with a smile.

She gave into the irresistible urge to return his smile. Underlying his super-patient attitude had been a glowing sense of pride in his accomplishment that a blind woman could not miss. It was sweet and she'd found it impossible to stay angry in the face of his obvious pleasure in her condition. Not that she was really angry anyway.

She was still hurting *and* feeling guilty because she hated the thought that in his mind her love wasn't real.

As reluctant as she was to give his view credence, she could see where he justified his belief.

She sighed.

"That is a sound I have come to dislike intensely."

Turning startled eyes to meet his now serious blue gaze, she asked, "What?" He hated her sighing? "Why?"

"It indicates an unhappiness in you I do not wish to be there." There was no evidence of his earlier light-hearted mood as he cupped her face in his hands. "We know how pleased I am about your pregnancy, but are *you* happy about the baby, *tesoro mio*?"

It was always so hard to concentrate when he touched her, but she made herself answer as prosaically as possible. "Yes, how can you doubt it?"

"You were frightened yesterday."

"I still am a little, but my head knows I shouldn't be and the thought of having your baby is a very sweet one, if you want the truth."

His hands dropped away and he sat back against the seat, his expression disbelieving. "So sweet, you do not wish to marry me."

"Can we not talk about that right now?" They'd been getting along so well and she didn't want to mar the pleasure of that rapport. She didn't like being at odds with him…she was used to her time with him being a source of pleasure, not pain. Even when they disagreed.

"Just accept that I am happy about the baby." Before he could say something cutting, she went on. "By all rights, you shouldn't be pleased that your secret lover is pregnant with your child, but you are and I accept that. I don't care if it makes sense in your brain that I'm content to be pregnant with your baby, or not. I am, all right?"

"I am glad."

She nodded. "Good."

"If you do not wish to discuss marriage…"

"I don't."

"Let us discuss you moving in with me."

"*What*?" The expression "jumping from the frying pan into the fire" sprang to mind.

"You are pregnant with my child."

"That's been well and truly established."

"Even if you do not wish to have a relationship with me, I want to look after you. Will you allow me that privilege?" He looked so serious…so determined.

But he'd picked her up wrong.

"You believe I don't want to have a relationship with you?"

"You said so. As you have pointed out repeatedly, you broke up with me."

Guilt flayed her and she didn't think he meant it to. He was right…but darn it, it wasn't because she hadn't wanted a relationship with him. It was because she'd wanted something more than he'd been prepared to give…because she'd wanted one for the right reasons.

He's prepared to give you what you want now, an insidious voice inside her head told her.

"I didn't break up with you because I didn't want you." She remembered what he'd said the night before about how he thought her willingness to do so meant she didn't really love him. "And it wasn't because I don't love you, either. It just hurt too much to be with you."

"As my *secret* lover?"

"Yes," she whispered painfully.

"But when I offered to remove the secret aspect, you still refused to be with me."

"Because I didn't want to hurt more down the road when you left."

"Not to be too repetitive, but that is no longer an issue. I want marriage. That is a permanent relationship."

"I want to believe that, but…"

"But you do not?"

"I want to," she said again.

He sighed. "But you do not trust me to remain faithful."

"I didn't say that."

"You do not have to. I have convinced you that I am not the faithful type."

"Well, actually, that summation of your character never rang true."

"But you do not believe our marriage will last a lifetime."

"How can it, with nothing but an unexpected pregnancy and your stubbornness to hold it together?"

"We have much more than that."

"Like what?"

"Like *your* stubbornness, for starters, and a white-hot passion that has not ebbed in six months, and a commitment to family and a desire for the same kind of future. We even work for the same company."

"Correction…you own the company I work for."

"But that is something in common, something that holds us together. We are both content to live in Sicily. That matters. Our marriage will last. We are both too strong and determined to allow anything else."

Was he right? She just didn't know, but one thing he said made a lot of sense. They were both very determined people.

She sighed.

He frowned. "You were not happy to wake up with me beside you in bed this morning."

But she had been when he insisted on her staying there while he got her toast and tea so her tummy would settle. She'd liked being looked after, especially by him.

"You surprised me." It sounded lame in the face of his certainty she didn't want to be with him, which was not the problem. "Everything is just happening so fast. I feel like my life has been changing with the regularity of a metronome and swinging just as drastically from one extreme to another too."

"But they are extremes you have instigated."

"I didn't get myself pregnant," she gasped, and glared at him.

He grinned, not in the least offended now that she had assured him she was happy about the baby. He looked supremely satisfied. "No, *amante*. *I* did that."

She couldn't help it. She burst out laughing.

For some reason her laughter triggered something in Marcello and before she knew what was happening, she was being kissed to within an inch of her life. He tasted so good and it felt so right to have his arms around her that she didn't even think to try to deny him. When he lifted his head, she was sitting securely on his lap and tingling in places she'd prefer not to talk about.

As if he could not help himself, he kissed her once more, hard and on the lips. "You taste good, *cara*."

"So do you." But she might respect herself a little more if she had at least minimal defenses against him.

"So, you will move in with me?"

She went to sigh and stopped herself. She wasn't unhappy, not really. And didn't want him thinking otherwise. She just knew when she was beaten. The truth was she was pregnant and feeling vulnerable and she'd rather live with him than fight the good fight by herself. Especially when she wasn't sure it was the *good* fight anymore.

"Well?" he demanded when she didn't answer right away.

"And what will you do if I refuse, move in with me?"

His expression gave him away.

"That was exactly what you had planned, wasn't it?"

"If you want separate beds," he said with what she thought was total overkill considering the fact that she was on his lap and making no moves to go anywhere, "then my place is the most logical. I have spare bedrooms."

She snuggled into him, laying her head on his chest. "That's good to know," she said punitively.

She could play cool, too.

CHAPTER TEN

"ARE you ready to go?"

Danette looked up from her computer. Marcello stood in her doorway looking so gorgeous her heart rolled. "I would have thought you had too much to do to leave on time tonight. We spent the morning in the doctor's office and the bookstore. Then you insisted on stopping for lunch before we came into work. I'm surprised your secretary isn't climbing the walls from canceling all the meetings you've missed."

He shrugged. "She is paid well to do what she does and my meetings can wait. The most pressing issues can be attended to from my study at home. I do no want to keep you in the office."

"Don't think you have to leave on my account. To tell you the truth, I've still got a ton of catching up to do myself."

He stepped into the room and shut the door. "I do not think working extra hours is a good idea. You need your rest."

"I'm pregnant, not sick, Marcello."

"Funny, I was sure you were sick when you went rushing for the restroom at the doctor's office this morning."

"Don't remind me. But I'm not feeling like that now and I'd rather work when I've got the energy for it."

"How much longer do you need?"

"Two or three hours."

He rolled his eyes and shook his head. "Do not push it, *cara*. Even prior to your pregnancy I did not approve of you working long into the evening. I will be back in ninety minutes, be prepared to go."

She might love him to death, but she wasn't about to let him start running every minute of her life. "I'm not going to be ready to leave in under two hours. You are of course welcome to go home without me."

"That is not going to happen."

"Then I will see you in two hours."

"Yes, you will."

"Your bossy nature is showing again," she informed him with interest.

He shrugged, a smile tugging at his lips as he turned to go. "And your stubborn streak is in full evidence, but I can deal with it, just as you will learn to deal with my so-called bossy tendencies."

"So long as you realize I reserve the right to return the favor, I'm sure you are right."

He stopped with his hand on the doorknob. "In what way?"

Clearly the idea of a woman getting bossy with him was a completely foreign concept. However, she had no doubts that Flavia had asserted her will with her son on more than one occasion, even if she'd been more subtle about it than Danette had the finesse or desire to be.

"If I think you are working too many hours, I will demand you go home," she warned him.

"I will remember that," he said, looking strangely pleased and not at all put out by the prospect, and then he left.

Ten minutes later, a young woman who worked in the company cafeteria arrived at Danette's desk with a tray of nutritious snacks and some bottled water, per Marcello's instructions.

"Did he order himself anything?" Danette asked.

"No, *signorina*," the young woman said, her eyes alight with curiosity about the employee the president of the company had taken precious time from his busy schedule to order food for.

"I see." She dug in her purse and pulled out some money and then handed it to the cafeteria worker. "Then please take him a bottle of fruit juice and a plate of snacks like the one you brought me."

"I do not know…"

"It's all right. Trust me." In the end, Danette was pretty positive it was the woman's curiosity that convinced her to do it rather than her assurances.

"Oh, and put this on it." She scribbled a quick note, folded it and handed it to the bemused cafeteria worker.

Ten minutes later the phone on her desk rang.

She picked it up. "Danette Michaels here."

"Thank you, *tesoro*."

She smiled and twisted the phone cord around her finger as she leaned back in her chair. "You're welcome. I appreciate your thinking of it to begin with."

Her tummy stayed more settled when she kept small amounts of food in it at all times. She'd learned that pretty quickly.

"I liked the note, too."

She'd written:

> Tit-for-tat.
> Love,
> Danette

"Did you?" She wondered which bit he'd appreciated the most, her subtle one-upmanship, or her avowal of love.

Probably the former, she conceded. He didn't believe she loved him, but she aimed to convince him otherwise. Even if he didn't love her, she realized she couldn't marry him with him believing her feelings for him were no more than physical lust and friendship. Which come to think of it was not a terrible definition of love, but it didn't stretch to explain a depth of feeling that made her certain she'd give her life for him, too.

"Yes. Be ready to go at seven."

"What will you do if I'm not?"

"Carry you out of your office."

She didn't doubt he meant it. "That might look a little odd to the other employees."

"I am not worried about it—are you?"

She knew what he was asking. They'd arrived at the building together that afternoon and he'd made no effort to hide the fact that they were very much together. Considering the rumors already rife because of her bout in the bathroom the day before, the company grapevine had no doubt drawn all the right conclusions plus some. She'd been getting odd looks all afternoon, but the truth was…she *didn't* care.

"I thought it would bother me more to have my co-workers know that you're my lover, but it doesn't. I know I'm good at my job and don't trade on our relationship. That's all that really matters."

"So, I *am* your lover?"

"Um…I don't understand the question."

"It is a matter of how many beds will be occupied in my home this night."

Crunch time. She hadn't expected to have to share her decision over the phone. "You seemed pretty intent on getting some use out of one of your spare bedrooms."

"If that is what you need to feel comfortable moving into my home, then so be it."

She didn't know what she needed. She wished she did, but realizing she was pregnant had muddled everything up in her brain and her heart was already a hopeless mess. "I like sleeping in your arms," she admitted.

"I, too, like this."

"I know, but…"

"But?" he asked, a tremendous amount of tension conveyed in that single word.

"I don't know if I'm ready to make love to you. If I did, you'd see it as capitulation. You'd start planning the wedding."

"You know me well."

"I suppose. In some ways."

"So, you would allow me to sleep next to you, but do not wish me to touch you intimately?"

"Yes, but…"

"Another but?"

"It isn't fair to you. I know you'd want to make love."

"I will take what I can get right now." He didn't sound happy, only resigned. But then he didn't sound super disappointed, either.

"Do you find my pregnancy a turn-off?"

"How can you ask me such a question?"

"Well, you're taking this better than I thought you would."

"Do I have a choice?"

"Only in the way you react, I guess."

"You guess?"

"I mean, I know what I need right now…"

"And that is?"

"Space."

"I cannot give you that."

"If you don't try to make love to me, that will be more space than I expected from you in your current territorial mood."

"You believe that my *territorial mood* as you put it is a result of your pregnancy?"

"Yes."

"Even though I did not want our relationship to end, prior to me finding out about it?"

He was right, that didn't make any sense, but… "It's all muddled in my head and sex will only make it worse. I'm sure of it."

"Maybe it would make it better. I know it would for me."

"No pressure. You promised."

"When did I promise?"

"Just now?" she asked, rather than stated, because she wasn't sure that's what he had done.

"I promised to sleep with you without touching you intimately."

"Yes."

"I did not promise to pretend I no longer want you. Indeed if I did, your active imagination would no doubt have you thinking all sorts of wrongheaded scenarios."

"It wouldn't!"

"You can say this after asking me if I no longer found you sexually irresistible because of your pregnancy, merely because I had not reacted with enough disappointment to your no sex edict?"

"Oh…well, I suppose. Do you think it's pregnancy or finally accepting I love you that has me so muddled?" she asked.

"Pregnancy." There was no doubt in his voice.

"I do love you," she said with a catch in her voice. "I wish you would believe me."

"Give me something to believe."

"Like what?"

"Like marriage."

She should have seen that coming. "Anything else?"

"What else is there? You refuse me the succor of your body and the comfort of giving you and our child my name. I do not mean to hurt you, Danette, but that is not a love I can recognize."

Her eyes began to burn. He didn't mean to hurt her, but his lack of belief hurt all the same. "I need to get back to work."

"Yes, I also."

"I…um…are you sure you're going to be okay with sleeping with me and not doing anything else? It's just not what you're used to," she babbled, not even sure what she was trying to say. "Even when it was that time of month for me, we never slept completely platonically."

And she was afraid that even the lightest caresses on his part would crumble her defenses against making love.

An explosion of air sounded at the other end of the line. "If you are that worried about sharing my bed, then it would be best if you stayed in the guest room. I do not wish to importune you in any way."

"I didn't mean—"

"Your meaning was clear. Do not let it concern you. I must go now. *Ciao, bella.*"

"*Ciao.*"

But she didn't work after hanging up the phone, not for several minutes, as she blinked back tears and mulled over what he had said. Obviously it was important to him that she sleep with him. Why couldn't she give him that much?

But she knew why. She couldn't trust her own shaky defenses where he was concerned. If they made love, for her it would be comfort…for him a commitment she was not yet ready to make.

CHAPTER ELEVEN

DANETTE woke after a less than satisfactory night in the guest room bed. Not that the bed was unsatisfactory in any way. Just like everything else in Marcello's four-bedroom apartment, it was top-notch. The mattress was comfortable, the decor in the bedroom peaceful and eye catching, but she missed Marcello.

They had eaten in relative silence the night before, their conversation, what there was of it, centered around the baby. Marcello had excused himself directly after dinner to catch up on work in his study and she had tried watching television for a while. He still hadn't come out of his study when she went to bed two hours later.

She ached from the distance she felt between them. It was worse than right after the breakup because her heart kept telling her that they *should* be together, they *could* be together, if not for her refusal.

She'd woken several times in the night, reaching for him only to find an empty bed. Had she been a fool to demand space that only seemed to hurt and add to her turmoil instead of making it easier to think, like it was supposed to? Was he right in thinking that making love would actually clarify their situation, not make it worse?

Talking was supposed to help, but it felt like all they did was talk in circles.

She wanted him to accept that she loved him *before* they got married. But from what she could tell, it was going to take her risking marriage to him for him to believe her feelings were real.

If he had demanded it as proof of her love, she would rebel. That kind of emotional blackmail left her cold.

But that wasn't what was happening. He was genuinely confused by her actions. Everything he did and said showed just how little he understood what motivated her. And how little he believed that motivation was anything resembling true love. Maybe Bianca had been better at showing her love than Danette was, but then the other woman had known she was loved in return. That made a huge difference and Danette was only beginning to see how stingy unrequited love could be.

But love shouldn't be selfish and it shouldn't hold back out of self-protection, either. In one respect, Marcello was very right. Love that was spoken, but not acted upon wasn't much of a love at all.

Love shouldn't make a woman a doormat, but it should make her strong enough to take risks she wouldn't otherwise take. Shouldn't it? Loving Marcello definitely shouldn't make her act in a way that hurt him, but that was exactly what had happened.

Her rejection had hurt him every bit as much as his desire to keep her a secret and never to marry her had hurt her. She had absolutely no doubts on that score and it made her feel terrible. She didn't want to hurt him.

Her thoughts were cut off by a vise squeezing tight

around her stomach and an urge to throw up that had her leaping from the bed and running to the en suite. She was retching, her face clammy and her whole body aching, when a warm hand settled on the small of her back.

"Why did you not wait for me? I was bringing you tea and toast."

"I didn't have a choice," she breathed, feeling shaky and light headed, but her stomach finally settled.

He made a noise that was part protest, part remorse and she turned her head to rest against his body kneeling so close to hers.

He cupped her cheek. "*Amante*, what am I going to do with you?"

"Help me stand up?" she asked in a voice that was shockingly weak.

He said nothing more until he had not only done that, but helped her rinse her mouth with water and then washed her face and neck with a cool cloth.

When he was done, he lifted her in his arms and carried her back into the bedroom. "If I had been here, I would have known the moment you woke and been able to take care of you. This sleeping in separate beds is foolish!"

She nibbled on a piece of dry toast and sipped at weak, but very sweet tea while he vented his frustration in a mixture of Italian, English and a couple of other languages she could only guess at.

He finally wound down and sat beside her on the bed, his usually immaculate appearance having taken a decided turn for the worse. His hair was mussed from running impatient fingers through it and he'd even loosened his tie and the top button on his dress shirt as if he'd needed more air.

He took her hand in his big tanned one, his fingers playing softly over the back of hers. "I apologize. I am going on like a madman and you are feeling ill. Forgive me."

"Wow. For a guy who doesn't say he's sorry very often, you're really good at it."

He grimaced. "Thank you. I think."

She smiled, feeling much better than she had been five minutes ago. "I think you're right though."

"*You think I am right?*" He sounded stunned. "About us not sleeping in separate beds?"

She nodded, making no sudden movements that might bring back the nausea. "I slept very poorly last night."

"You missed me?" Satisfaction gleamed in his blue gaze.

She had to stifle her own humor at his reaction. She didn't think he would understand it, but humility simply was not his thing. "Yes."

"I missed you, too, *tesoro*."

"So…um…no more separate beds."

"You are sure?"

"Positive."

"And your concern I will try to seduce you?"

"I trust you."

"That is something."

Yes, it was. But was it enough?

She got her first personal taste of the intrusiveness of the press an hour later when she answered the phone in her office to discover a reporter who wanted a quote on her relationship with Marcello at the other end of the line. She hung up after a firm, "No comment," and stopped answering the outside line on her phone altogether after the third such call.

Voice mail was a wonderful thing.

She really appreciated the fact that Marcello lived in a high security building with underground parking, and that Scorsolini Shipping also had underground parking and a crack security force. Somehow, word of her relationship with Marcello had gotten out and she had no desire to run a gauntlet of reporters to and from their car.

She wondered how he was handling the media attention. It was the one thing he'd made it very clear he did not want to deal with. And now they were smack in the middle of it. She shuddered to think what would happen when the press learned about the baby.

A light rap sounded on her open office door and she looked up.

Lizzy came in, a grin on her face and her eyes lit with curiosity. "So, what is this I hear about you and the big boss having a thing?"

"Um…what did you hear?"

"Come on, Danette. It's all over the place. You moved in with him and everything. I can't believe I didn't guess. Did it happen that night at the restaurant? But then how would you have gotten pregnant so fast?"

"Pregnant?" she asked faintly.

Lizzy just looked at her. Danette had known word would spread around the company, so she needed to just bite the bullet and come clean with her friend. "We've been going out for a while."

"In secret?" Lizzy asked with awe.

"Yes. Neither one of us wanted our relationship to become public knowledge." Now was not the time to explain that the relationship, such that it was, wasn't actually on anymore.

After agreeing to share his bed, even platonically, she wasn't sure that was true anyway.

"I understand." Lizzy leaned on the other side of Danette's desk. "It's going to make it a bit awkward for you around here, but you're fab at your job and everybody knows it, and you're definitely strong enough to handle what little flack may come your way."

"Thanks for the vote of confidence." Danette smiled.

"So, are you really pregnant?" Lizzy whispered.

Danette nodded.

Lizzy squealed and came around the desk to hug her. "Congratulations, *chica*! That's wonderful news! I'm so happy for you!"

Danette laughed and hugged her friend back. "Thanks. I'm pretty happy about it."

"Not when you're puking, I bet you're not."

"It comes with the territory."

"I won't ask when the wedding is because I don't want to accidentally let it slip and be responsible for the news cameras showing up, but I just want you to know I'm really, really, really happy for you."

Lizzy's visit left Danette in high spirits and she was powering through her to-do list and doing a fair job of ignoring the messages left by reporters on her voice mail when a representative for an exclusive boutique arrived in her office. The woman looked more like a cover model than a boutique employee and explained she was there to show Danette a selection of clothing for her upcoming trip to Isole dei Re.

"I have several outfits per the prince's instructions

here," she said, indicating a portable clothes rack she'd rolled into Danette's office.

"Marcello sent you?" Danette asked.

The other woman nodded even as Danette was picking up her phone to dial Marcello's private line.

He picked up on the second ring. "What is it, Danette?"

"There's some kind of personal shopper woman here—in my *office*. She wants me to look at clothes, Marcello. Why is she here?"

"I want to fly directly to Scorsolini Island after work today. Our takeoff slot is for four-thirty."

"What? You want to fly out early? Why?"

"My father wants to spend some time getting to know you before my brother's wedding."

Remembering what he had told her about Maggie Thomson's first meeting with the king, Danette did not smile at the prospect. "Oh."

"It is important to me, *amante*."

"Then we will go of course."

"Good. We can fly to the States in order for me to meet your parents after the wedding."

"All right." She hadn't even told them she was dating, much less that she was pregnant. She'd have to do it from Isole dei Re because they wouldn't even be out of bed before she and Marcello flew out. "But that still doesn't explain the personal shopper with her rack of elegant clothes."

She gave the boutique employee an apologetic smile for talking about her as if she wasn't there.

"I knew you would not want to take time off from work to pack, and assumed you would refuse to leave with me if you did not have some clothes and an appropriate outfit to wear for the wedding."

"And this is your idea of a preemptive strike to gain my compliance?"

"Yes. Does that bother you?"

She looked at the three outfits the woman had turned to hang face out, and had to shake her head. "How can it? She's got impeccable taste."

"Both my mother and Therese favor that boutique."

"Then I guess I'm in good company, but what about my toothbrush?" she asked facetiously.

"All personal toiletries have been taken care of."

"Thank you. I guess I'd better take care of the clothes thing so I can get back to work."

"You do not sound overly excited about it."

"It beats shopping by regular means, that's for sure."

Marcello laughed. "We will leave for the airport at three. Be ready."

"Yes, sir."

"Tease me at your peril, *tesoro*."

"What will you do about it?"

"That is for me to know and you to worry about."

"Note, I'm not worried."

"You are relying on the pregnancy card here?"

"Maybe…"

His laughter lifted her spirits as high as Lizzy's visit had.

"I'll see you later, *caro*."

There was silence for a few seconds and she thought they'd somehow been disconnected, but then he said, "Until then, *cara*," in a voice that sent tingles clear to her toes.

The man was definitely lethal. She'd be doing the sanity of women everywhere a favor by taking him off the market.

With that tantalizing thought playing over in her mind, she selected four outfits and answered a list of personal preference questions for the boutique. Then the personal shopper left after promising to have everything packed in a set of luggage and transported to Marcello's jet at the airport.

Danette wasn't entirely sure why four outfits required an entire set of luggage, but she had too much to do for a sales report due later that afternoon to spend any time thinking about it.

Marcello hung up the phone with a smile on his face. No way could she know about the stories in the tabloid press. She sounded too natural. Too relaxed. He did not think she would respond so carelessly to some of the ugly innuendo and downright provocative assertions being made.

His decision to leave early for Isole dei Re had been the right one. She needed to be protected and he would protect her. Always.

He glared down at the offending tabloids spread across his desk. They had been waiting for him when he arrived at work that morning. Some would not hit the newsstands until the next day, but they all had something in common…they implied things that would hurt Danette. And she had been hurt enough.

It had never been his intention to cause her pain, but he had. It made him angry that he hadn't seen the toll the secrecy of their relationship would take on her eventually. Because other women did not interest him, he assumed pictures of him with them would not bother her. He had been wrong.

And he understood how wrong after seeing her that

night with Ramon. He had to admit to himself that if she had been dancing with the other man, blood probably would have been shed.

It was a good thing that hadn't happened. There was enough ugly speculation surrounding their relationship. His fury at the press was barely containable, but mixed with it was a surprise.

He felt no personal embarrassment at the headlines proclaiming him everything from a cuckolded boy-friend to a emotionless seducer who had taken advantage of his role as president of the company. He simply didn't care, but the knowledge those same headlines would hurt Danette ripped at his gut.

He would not allow her to see them, and if it took an extended stay behind the walls of their palace in Isole dei Re to protect her, that was what they would do.

Danette assumed Marcello didn't want to discuss the fact that the press were obviously on to their relation-ship because he didn't bring the matter up during the drive to the airport or their flight to Isole dei Re. It was a long flight and they both spent the first couple of hours working. Then they had dinner and Marcello went back to work, but suggested she relax and watch a movie on the personal DVD player.

What she really wanted was a nap, and she fell asleep halfway through her movie.

Danette was sleeping when they touched down and only woke up when Marcello gently shook her shoulder. "We are arrived, *amante*."

She blinked her eyes, trying to focus. "Okay. Um…what time is it?"

"Close to 3:00 a.m. in our time zone and about nine in the evening in Paradiso."

"Okay." She was so tired, she just wanted to go back to sleep.

He smiled. "You are really out of it, aren't you?"

She nodded. He laughed, and the next thing she knew she was being lifted from her seat, high into his arms, and being carried off the plane. When he ignored her sleepy protest that she could walk on her own, she laid her head against his shoulder and dozed. She was vaguely aware of being placed in a car and of a short ride before the car stopped.

Once again Marcello carried her. This time, she didn't even make a token protest, but wrapped her arms around his neck and snuggled into him. He said something to someone else as his arms tightened their hold on her.

Suddenly lights blazed against her eyelids and she blinked her eyes open to look around her. There was Italian marble everywhere, and large Roman-style columns as well as statuary that rivaled anything she'd seen on her trip to Florence the first month she started working at Scorsolini Shipping.

"Looks like a museum."

A deep, masculine laugh sounded from behind her. "Yes, perhaps it does."

She turned her head and beheld the king of Isole dei Re. She was too sleepy to be overwhelmed. She simply stared at him.

"Hello, Danette Michaels. I hear you are pregnant with the next Scorsolini grandchild."

She glared up at Marcello. "You told him, too?"

"You expected him not to? I assure you, after reading today's papers I would have been aware anyway."

"*Papa.*"

Something passed between the men that she was too rummy to get, but the king shook his head. "She will learn eventually."

"The only thing I want to learn right now is where I'm supposed to sleep," she mumbled and then realizing how horribly rude that sounded, she blushed to the roots of her hair. "I'm sorry. I didn't mean…"

"Do not worry, child. Marcello's mother was the same way when she was pregnant with him."

"What way is that?"

"Cranky and easily tired."

"I'm not cranky." She looked at Marcello, her eyes going misty for no apparent reason. "Am I cranky?"

"No, *tesoro*. You are fine." The glare he gave his father could have singed brick.

"Flavia was very emotional, too. I did not mean to offend you, little one. Please forgive an old man his less than tactful tongue."

"Not old," she mumbled against Marcello's chest. "But definitely tactless."

She thought she'd said it too low for him to hear, but the sound of the older man's laughter followed them up the stairs. At least he hadn't been offended.

She awoke the next morning to gentle prodding from Marcello. He had a delicate china cup of steaming tea in his hand. "I hoped if you had your tea and toast right on waking, you would not get sick."

"It's worth a try." And surprisingly, it worked. Her nausea never made it past the point of discomfort and by the time she was done with her toast, it was gone completely.

She was feeling quite decent when she followed

Marcello down the marble staircase and along several long corridors that made her feel like Alice in Wonderland. "It really is a palace, isn't it?"

"Naturally. What else would a royal family live in?"

"But you're all so normal."

"In some ways, of course, we are like anyone else. But there is a responsibility to our birth that changes us and the way we must live our lives."

Was he trying to explain the secrecy thing again? He shouldn't have to, she was finally ready to admit. After all, she had been more than okay with it at first. It was just that as her love grew her ability to keep it hidden diminished. And the need to do so started to hurt.

Well, okay, and dancing with blondes was out. Forever.

Only, surrounded by the trappings of Marcello's royal birth, she thought maybe she was beginning to understand what motivated him a little better. Both in regards to their relationship and the baby.

They found his father in a large room that was imposing not only for its size but the opulence of its decor.

"I feel like we're in the Vatican," she whispered to Marcello. "I'm afraid to sit down and be thought disrespectful."

A deep laugh she remembered from the night before sounded from the other side of the room. "Maggie told Tomasso the same thing, he said."

"You heard me?" Oh, great. It wasn't like she hadn't been outspoken enough the night before.

King Vincente sat on a throne. A real live throne. It was huge, like thrones should be, she supposed. Made of dark, ornately carved mahogany and the royal crest above his head gilded in gold. Oh, goodness. The throne and the man were both incredibly impressive.

His eyes were the same blue as Marcello's and though there was silver in his hair, he was drop-dead gorgeous. Just like his son.

He smiled, showing even, white teeth. "The acoustics in this room were designed so that when my ancestors entertained they could easily keep track of conversations from every direction, but you will note that in order for you to hear me, I must project my voice."

"This is the formal receiving room," Marcello added.

"But it has a throne…I thought that made it the throne room."

"No." Marcello led her to a seat on a pristine white Queen Anne style chair near his father's throne. Three dozen or so of them lined the walls in the immediate vicinity of the throne. "The official throne room is much more ostentatious, to impress visiting dignitaries. This room has a more prosaic purpose."

"More ostentatious?" She wasn't sure she was ready to see the other room.

This one was impressing her to death…and intimidating her a little, too. She was really glad Marcello was the third son and not the first.

King Vincente laughed and Marcello nodded. "Yes, very much so. I will show you later. Tradition dictates that my father meet with his subjects in this room every Friday, all day long."

"The first visitors will be admitted in one hour's time," King Vincente added.

"Every Friday? That makes you a pretty accessible king, doesn't it?" Danette asked.

"That was the intent of my forefathers. They did not want the unrest often encountered in the City States that then comprised Italy, nor the deep distrust that developed between the monarchy and the parliament in England."

"That was smart of them."

"Yes, but then there is no doubting my ancestors were brilliant men."

She laughed out loud and turned to face Marcello who had taken a seat beside her after greeting his father with the customary kiss on both cheeks. "It definitely comes from both sides of your family."

"What does?" King Vincente asked.

Marcello's smile was warm and sent a sense of well-being spreading through her. "Danette considers me arrogant."

"And you believe he gets this trait from both his mother and myself?" King Vincente asked her.

"I'm sure of it."

"You find Flavia arrogant?"

"Had she been a shy retiring little thing, I'm sure she would never have interested you," Danette replied by way of compromise. She didn't know if he would find her assessment of his former wife flattering, or not.

Something told her he was not tolerant of any criticism directed at his family and that included the woman who had had the temerity to divorce him.

"This is true," he mused, his expression giving nothing away regarding what he thought of her comment. "And was it *your* arrogance that drew my son's interest?"

She stared at him, not sure what to say. She'd never considered herself arrogant, but wouldn't it sound self-serving to say so? Especially after teasing both Marcello and his father about the fact that they were?

She hadn't meant to give offense, but neither did she think either man could even begin to deny the claim.

"She is not arrogant, Papa. Stubborn, yes. Proud as well, but she is far too compassionate with others to be arrogant."

"You say she is compassionate?" King Vincente asked with a wholly unexpected scathing disbelief and Danette flinched.

What had she done to give him such a low opinion of her?

"Yes, she is."

"And you," he asked, meeting Danette's gaze. "Do you consider yourself compassionate?"

"Yes, but why are you asking me that?"

"You refuse to marry my son."

"I didn't…I don't—"

"Papa, do not get into this right now," Marcello said in a voice that could have flash-frozen lava.

But King Vincente ignored him, his attention fixed wholly on Danette, his eyes raking her with disapproval. "You are willing to bring a child of Scorsolini blood into the world without the benefit of matrimony. The newspapers are slaying Marcello, making him out to be a fool and worse."

Marcello jumped to his feet, yelling at his father to shut up, but King Vincente went on remorselessly.

"You allow this vilification by the press of my son and know it will be no better for your child—yet you continue to deny Marcello his right to give you his name. How do you call that compassionate?" he demanded, his scorn withering her.

"I brought her here to be protected, not browbeaten," Marcello gritted out between clenched teeth as he grabbed her upper arms and lifted her from the chair. "You will not speak to my woman this way. Come, Danette, we will leave."

"Is she yours?" King Vincente demanded mockingly and she felt Marcello flinch, even though she knew he didn't want her to.

"It appears I have arrived just in time."

Another voice intruded, that of Flavia Scorsolini, and the effect it had on the king was electric.

CHAPTER TWELVE

THAT vaunted arrogance drained away along with the color in his face. His head snapped sideways. "*Flavia*?"

"As you see." She came forward and hugged both Marcello's rigidly furious form and Danette.

She patted Marcello's cheek. "Relax, my son. Do not be so angry with your papa. He wants only to protect you as you wish to protect Danette."

"I am no child to be protected!"

"You will always be our child. Accept it." She smiled at Danette, her eyes filled with warm understanding. "Do you wish to leave, *cara*?"

"No." The king had made some comments that she wanted explained and she wasn't going anywhere until they were.

"You see, Marcello? She is not ready to go."

"I will not allow her to be hurt."

"Some things cannot be hidden from her," was his mother's enigmatic reply.

Marcello looked entirely unconvinced and Danette pressed her hand over his heart. "Please, Marcello."

"I do not want you upset."

"Thank you, but I want to stay."

He stared at her, his eyes filled with some unnameable emotion. Finally he nodded and then turned his gaze to Flavia. "Mama, we did not expect you."

"I learned yesterday evening from the owner of my favorite boutique that you planned to fly over early. I guessed your reasoning, what your father's reaction to it would be, and changed my own plans accordingly."

"You think Miss Michaels needs your championship?" King Vincente asked in a voice that sounded strained.

Danette looked at him and sucked in a breath. He was watching Flavia with an expression so akin to agonized need that Danette's heart squeezed on his behalf.

Flavia appeared oblivious. "I think that you will browbeat the poor child out of that arrogance that up until now she has found rather amusing."

"Do you deny that her refusal to marry our son is detrimental to the welfare of everyone involved?"

"And did your son tell you that Danette refused to marry him?"

Anger replaced the strange expression on the king's face. "I read the papers. Nowhere was there a mention of an upcoming marriage. I know my son. He would never allow his child to enter the world without the benefit of his name. If there is no marriage planned, it is because she has refused him."

Flavia shook her head. "There is no fool like an old fool."

"I am not old," he said, sounding thoroughly outraged.

"But you are a fool."

King Vincente looked ready to spit nails, but he didn't yell. Danette found that fascinating.

"What newspapers?" she asked.

"The ones my son hoped to hide from you by coming here," Flavia replied.

"And it damn well would have worked if Papa had kept his big mouth shut."

"Marcello! I did not raise you to speak with such language or so disrespectfully to your father."

Marcello's glare gave no quarter, but Danette wasn't interested in family dynamics at the moment. "I repeat…what newspapers? Do you have copies?"

"Yes," King Vincente said at the same time Marcello growled, "No!"

Danette ignored the man she loved in favor of giving his father a gimlet stare. "I want to know what is being said. I want to see the papers, and I want to see them right now."

Marcello pulled her around to face him, his blue gaze more than a little troubled. "Danette, seeing the stories will serve no purpose but to hurt you. I do not want that."

"I know, but I can't hide from it. Your mom is right."

"No, she is wrong."

"I'm no wimp, Marcello. Either you trust me to handle the tough stuff, or you don't."

"And if I don't?"

"You do," she said with bone-deep certainty.

He didn't want her to see the stories, but he didn't doubt her ability to deal with them. She could see it in his eyes.

"I do."

Just then a young man in a business suit appeared beside King Vincente. "You buzzed me, Your Highness?"

"Bring me the papers with my son's picture plastered all over the front of them."

"This is foolish," Marcello ground out, but without much heat.

King Vincente frowned at him. "She has a right to know what is being said and if she is not strong enough to deal with it, she is not strong enough to be your princess."

"I'm not weak," Danette insisted, her own voice as heated as Marcello's had been earlier.

She'd spent her childhood being forced to submit to a bodily infirmity. She had fought, and won that fight. She would never submit willingly to any weakness again.

Flavia shook her head, making a clucking sound. "Vincente, I swear you grow only more stubborn and opinionated with age."

"Do you disagree with me?" he demanded with an edge that said her opinion really mattered.

"No, but if you had an ounce of sensitivity, you could have put it differently. Nor do I doubt this woman's strength."

"So, I am not a diplomat with my family," the older man grumbled. "A man should have some people in his life with whom he can be honest without fear of reprisal. Even a king."

"Yes, but some honesty is better left unspoken."

The aide returned with the papers and Danette looked through them while Marcello smoldered beside her. The headlines were vicious and the story copy wasn't much better.

"Prince's Secret Mistress Pregnant, But Is It Really His Baby?" read one. She winced when she read the next: "Sterile Prince To Be Father At Last… Or Is He?" Then there was, "Playboy Prince Has No Plans To Marry Pregnant Lover."

"I didn't realize they knew about the baby."

"Our trip to the bookstore was not the smartest move I have ever made," Marcello admitted in a roughened undertone.

But it wasn't just their reading material that had tipped off the press. Someone at Scorsolini Shipping had heard about her trip to the ladies' room during her presentation and about the employees from the warehouse who were commissioned to move her things from her little cottage to his big apartment.

Whoever it was had put the facts together correctly and tipped off the press. A sense of betrayal washed over her. It was hard to believe a co-worker would sell her and Marcello out like that.

She skimmed the articles and felt bile rise in her throat. The speculation ran all the way from the baby being someone else's to her refusing to marry because he'd already moved onto another woman before she discovered her pregnancy. The picture of him dancing with the blonde played prominently. So did old pictures of him with Bianca, and new ones of Danette and Marcello together coming out of the bookstore.

Unflattering comparisons were made between the two women and Danette's unsuitability for being the mother of a prince's baby was touted by more than one reporter. Her mother was going to have a fit for more reason than one when she read the article…if she read it. Danette sincerely hoped her mom didn't.

But the worst by far were the innuendos that implied she'd gotten pregnant by someone else and was trying to trap Marcello into marriage or bilk him for money.

She dropped the paper and said, "I think I'm going to be sick."

Marcello went to pick her up, but Flavia was faster, pushing Danette onto a short white sofa that matched the chairs in the reception hall. "Lie back. Yes, just like that. Now breathe deeply and concentrate on something else."

Danette did the breathing, but she couldn't think of anything but the horrible things said in those articles. She turned stricken eyes to Marcello. "I'm sorry. I didn't mean—"

"None of this was your fault," he said fiercely, dropping to his knees beside her.

But it was. She'd worried what would happen when the press knew about the baby and now she knew. It was awful. "You hate this…this is what you wanted to avoid more than anything. I'm so sorry," she said again, knowing the words were inadequate for the way his pride had to have been savaged by those stories. "You don't doubt you are the father, do you?"

"How can you ask me that? I have already said I had no worries on that score."

"But now that all this has come out…"

"Make no mistake, I hate those stories and the attention is unpleasant, but my thought since reading the first one yesterday morning has been to protect you. I do not care what they say about me. I know that baby inside you is mine."

"It is, Marcello."

"Of course he knows it is." Flavia shook her head and patted Danette's hand. "My son is no fool…usually."

"And what is that supposed to mean?" King Vincente asked with umbrage.

Flavia spun to face him. "You can take full credit for his idiocy, too. Because he was already married and loved once before, he convinced Danette that he is no more capable of fidelity than you are."

The king had looked pale before, but he looked positively gray now. "I—"

"You have to stop punishing yourself. Do you hear me? You have planted this stupid idea into the heads of our sons, and the good God above alone knows how much damage it has done with the older boys."

"Your Highness, the people are awaiting entry outside the doors." The aide had come back.

"I must do my duty," King Vincente said, his expression of a man who was going through hell and saw no way out.

Flavia nodded, her expression unreadable. "Of course. Marcello, bring Danette. We will retire to the private apartments." She yawned delicately. "I could use a nap. I flew through the night and got very little sleep."

"You could have flown with us," Marcello said as he helped Danette to her feet and led both women from the big reception room through a door in the back.

"I did not learn of your departure until after the fact."

Marcello put his arm around Danette's waist, guiding her toward the door behind the throne his mother had come in through.

Danette stopped at the door and turned to look back at the king. "I didn't know about the articles."

He grimaced. "So I saw. I am sorry for my earlier accusations."

"I don't want to hurt Marcello."

"And he does not want to hurt you, but as Flavia and I learned, good intentions are not always enough."

Danette impulsively ran back into the room and put

her hand on the king's arm. She wanted to hug him, but didn't have the nerve. "It's going to be all right."

His gorgeous blue eyes were filled with an old sadness. "I hope you are right."

"Trust me and trust your son. He's a good man."

"Yes, he is. A better man than his father."

"I don't know. I think you must be pretty special to have raised Marcello the way he is."

"Flavia had more to do with that than I did."

Danette smiled and gave into the urge to hug the intimidating older man. King or not, he was hurting. She spoke near his ear. "It was a joint effort and you may as well accept it. Ditch the humble bit, it doesn't suit you."

He laughed and she stepped back.

"I believe you will make a very good princess, Danette Michaels."

Danette smiled, warmed by the vote of confidence. "Thank you."

He pulled her into an embrace, kissing both her cheeks, and tears stung her eyes for no apparent reason. She stepped back and turned to go, but then stopped and leaned toward him to whisper.

"A small piece of advice? When a woman stands up for you like Flavia just did—she doesn't hate your guts."

King Vincente's jaw dropped and Danette rushed to catch up with Marcello.

"Come," Flavia said and Marcello pulled Danette through the door, closing it firmly behind them.

"Come for a walk with me on the grounds," Marcello said after they left Flavia at her rooms so she could take the nap she said she wanted.

"I'd like that."

He took her out into a formal garden that looked like

it had come right out of a Renaissance painting. "It's gorgeous out here."

"I have always enjoyed it."

"But you chose to live in Sicily rather than here on Scorsolini Island when you came of age."

"Yes."

"Why?"

"I wanted to be near Mama, and I wanted to make my own mark on the world. Besides, Papa wanted me in Sicily looking after Mama."

Danette nodded. She had no problem believing that.

"Why did you want to hide the stories from me?" she asked, cutting to the heart of what they needed to deal with.

"I knew they would upset you and I was right."

"But they upset you, too."

"You are my woman. It is my job to protect you."

"It's my job to protect you, too."

"Is it?" He smiled down at her winsomely. "There are other things I would prefer you spent your time doing."

Remembering the entire set of luggage loaded onto the plane for her benefit she said, "You didn't plan on going back to Sicily right away, did you?"

"No. I thought a long visit here would protect you from the brunt of the media frenzy, but my parents thought differently."

"Please don't be angry with either of them. They are only doing what they think is right."

"And what do you think is right?"

"Knowing, no matter how much it hurts, is better than being ignorant." She bit her lip and then asked, "Would there be as much of a story if we were getting married?"

He shrugged. "The lack of a marriage is gossip fodder,

to be sure, but it would be no guarantee against more stories. I learned that to my detriment with Bianca."

"Even so, I'm surprised you haven't used the stories to press your advantage in getting me to marry you. You had to know I would feel badly about them. Instead you tried to hide them from me."

"I did not want you hurt."

And maybe part of him didn't want her to see all the vicious things being written about him, either. She certainly hated knowing he'd read the stuff speculating that she'd been unfaithful to him and that the baby belonged to someone else.

"And to use the articles as leverage with you would be using emotional blackmail and I refuse to do that to you. Ever. It is a promise I made to you."

"I don't remember that promise," she said.

"That is because I did not make it out loud."

Oh, gosh…she was going to cry and really that shouldn't be happening. "That's really sweet," she choked out.

He sighed. "Tomasso warned me, and so did Papa actually."

"Warned you?" She swiped surreptitiously at her eyes. "About what?"

"Pregnant women have a tendency to cry over very small things."

"It's not a small th-thing t-to me that y-you are s-so honorable," she said, trying to breathe between words and not make her tears any more obvious than they needed to be.

He stopped and pulled her around to face him with gentle hands. "Shh…*tesoro*. It is all right. That I am an honorable man, this is a good thing, no?"

"Yes," she said in a wobbly voice.

"And you are an honorable woman."

"Y-yes…I think so."

"I know so."

"But maybe your dad is right. My refusal to marry you is selfish when I th-think of wh-what our child could face with the media."

"You are not selfish. Merely frightened and confused by too many changes coming at once."

"I'm not stupid."

"I never said you were. You were smart enough to date me—that shows a better than average IQ, does it not?"

She laughed as she was meant to, but her mind was spinning with the knowledge that she *had* to marry him. It was the right thing to do, and royalty were not the only people in the world who knew something about duty. Besides, marrying the man she loved was not exactly a hardship.

She'd told him she wasn't stupid. And waiting around for a romantic proposal from a guy whose whole reason for wanting to marry her was to secure his child's future and his role as a full-time papa would indeed be idiotic.

He wasn't going to all of a sudden realize he loved her, and she finally admitted that was what she'd been waiting for. Not just for him to accept her love, but for him to return it, and that wasn't fair. He gave her everything he could and demanding more wasn't going to make life for their baby or themselves any better.

She gripped his arms, her mouth going dry as she prepared to say what needed saying. "I'm smart enough to know that marriage between us makes a lot of sense and that the sooner we start making plans for it, the better off we all are. I suppose a small wedding like Tomasso and Maggie's makes the most sense, too."

Marcello stilled. "You are agreeing to marry me?"

"Yes."

He kissed her, his mouth devouring hers with a desperate passion that found a response in her own heart.

When she was trembling and plastered against him, he lifted his head. "There will be no small wedding. My mother and you have convinced me that only a traditional Sicilian ceremony will do."

"But the sooner we get married, the better."

"The delay of one month or even two will not harm anything."

Danette's mother would be very happy to hear that, and so she thought would Flavia. Perhaps the announcement of an upcoming wedding would be enough to declaw some of the nastier paparazzi predators. "If you're sure."

He frowned, his arms tightening around her. "You are being much too diffident...I do not recognize this side of you."

"Those stories in the tabloids were so awful, Marcello."

"But they mean nothing to us, because we know the truth. I do not care what they say so long as you agree to be mine."

She felt more emotion welling and buried her face in his chest so he wouldn't see it. "Your father's right, you know?"

"My father is lucky. I would have stayed angry with him for a good year over his stunt this morning, but I am too happy at your agreement to be my wife to remain angry. He should thank his lucky stars and his newest daughter-to-be."

"He was still right. I am arrogant." She sighed and nuzzled Marcello's warm, muscular chest. "I was so sure that keeping our relationship a secret wasn't necessary, but I realize now that it would have been awful if the press had gotten wind of it before."

"No worse than now."

"Not a lot could be worse than what they are saying now, but *before* you didn't know you wanted to marry me, and I think you would have felt obliged once ugly stories started to circulate."

"This is true. I would have felt the need to protect you, as I do now."

"I admire that, Marcello, I really do."

"And I admire your strength, both in refusing me until you were sure and in accepting me for the sake of our child's future." He kissed the top of her head, his hands warm on her back. "You are a very special woman, Danette."

"Thank you."

"I have a deep need to make love to my fiancée. Is that permissible?"

"More than permissible. It is desired."

They saw no one on the way to their royal apartments and he closed the door firmly behind them after they got inside. Then he locked it. "No interruptions."

She smiled, desire coiling tight in her belly. It had been too long. "Exactly what I had in mind."

"Which should tell you something."

"What?"

"That we are a good match."

"Because we both want privacy for making love? I hate to tell you this, but lots of men and women have the same requirement."

He smiled. "You can be a real smart mouth, you know that?"

She laughed. "It's part of my charm."

"Yes, it is. I meant because we so often think along the same paths. We belong together, *amante*. Do not doubt it."

"If I did, do you think I would have agreed to the marriage?"

"Yes." He went very serious. "For the sake of our child you would, but you have nothing to fear in accepting my proposal. Our marriage will be a good one. I promise you."

It didn't bother him that she was marrying him for the sake of the baby. None of the feelings of turmoil she was experiencing showed on his face. He looked supremely happy by her acquiescence. She wished she was so sanguine and she was going to try to be.

He might be marrying her for the sake of the baby, too, but that didn't mean he wouldn't be a good husband. "No more dancing with gorgeous blondes?" she asked just for good measure.

"I have already promised this, but make no mistake —no woman is as beautiful to me as you are."

"Not even Bianca?" She wanted to cut her tongue out the minute the words left her mouth.

As mood killers went, that had to be a classic. Worse, it made her sound like an insecure weakling, and she wasn't. She didn't need to be his first and best love to have a good relationship with him. As long as he stayed away from other live women, she could leave the dead one alone.

Couldn't she?

Surprisingly Marcello didn't look in the least annoyed. His expression was filled with an emotion she didn't understand when he cupped her face with his big, masculine hands. "Bianca has been gone for four years. You are very much alive. Your beauty to me is incomparable in *every* way."

"That's so sweet," she said, as those stupid pregnancy hormones made her eyes smart again.

He shook his head and then lowered it so their mouths were almost touching. "Not sweet. Truth. Accept now that I will never lie to you, or even exaggerate for a good cause. You can trust me completely."

"I want to. I'm marrying you," she reminded both of them.

"And you will never regret that choice. I guarantee it." His mouth sealed the words to her lips in a kiss unlike anything they had shared before.

She could taste his desire, but there was something else there, too. A tenderness she thought was probably because she was pregnant with his baby. She was no longer his illicit lover in a passionate affair, but the mother of his child who had just consented to marry him.

That made her special.

She responded with all the pent-up love in her soul, giving him back tenderness for tenderness and passion for passion. Everything else faded from her consciousness except for the feel of his lips on hers and his hands holding her face with such poignant possessiveness.

He licked along the seam of her lips and she opened her mouth, wanting his entry.

Their tongues teased one another and something that had been tight inside her heart since the break-up began to loosen. This man belonged to her on a fundamental level that denied the importance of declared love and emotions that could not be measured.

He was hers.

She was his.

They belonged to each other in an intimacy that no one else could share. The knowledge had been there in the back of her mind since the beginning. It was why she had not kicked him out the night she'd seen the picture of him with the blonde. Because the picture had shown a woman enjoying herself and a man smiling, but that man had been holding himself apart from the other woman. Danette had not realized it at first, not consciously. But she did now, in this moment of odd clarity.

He had denied her in the restaurant, but he could not deny her on an instinctive level. Ramon had seen Marcello's claim on her and so had Flavia. Danette had been too hurt to recognize it, but she knew it had been there. Just as the pain of seeing her with another man had been there.

"I didn't go out with Ramon to prove a point," she said against his lips.

Marcello reared back as if she'd struck him, his hands dropping from her face, his eyes for once perfect reflections of the maelstrom of emotion going through him. "What?"

"I wasn't trying to teach you an object lesson. How could I be? I didn't even know you would come to the restaurant that night."

"You *wanted* to go out with him?" Marcello asked in a hoarse voice that hurt her to hear.

"No."

"What are you saying then?"

"Lizzy tricked me into meeting them. I thought it was just going to be her and me, but she'd invited her boyfriend and Ramon along. She thought I needed to get out more. She didn't know about you. She thought I was lonely and she cared enough about me to try to fix that, but she knew I would have said no if she'd asked."

"She knew that because you'd said no before," he guessed.

"Yes."

"Our secrecy hurt you more than I knew."

"Yes." She couldn't deny it.

"I did not know that it hurt you at all. Please believe that."

"I do." She sighed. "You're not a sadist."

"It goes far deeper than that, if you could but see it. I never wanted you to be hurt by your association with me, but I could not walk away from you. I tried. It did not work."

"Rampant lust gone mad."

"It is more than lust."

She smiled, agreeing. Much more than lust now. "Yes, I am pregnant with your child."

"It was more than lust before you told me of your pregnancy."

She turned away, suddenly hurting in a way she didn't want him to see. She loved him. She would always love him and whatever he felt for her, no matter how much more it was than simple physical passion, it was not love. It never could be. She was not Bianca.

His hands curled around her waist and his mouth pressed against the sensitive skin of her nape. "I love you, Danette."

She tore from his arms, stepping back and turning on him, her heart slamming in her chest. "Don't say that! You don't mean it!"

His expression was fierce. "I do mean it."

"You can't. You just think you have to love the mother of your child. That's all it is, misplaced chivalry, but I don't want it. I can handle honesty between us. I can't handle that."

He glared and crossed the room with the speed of a predator, grabbing her wrists and pulling her body close to his. "You say you can handle honesty, then let us be honest. No woman has shared my bed for longer than two nights since Bianca's death and there were very few that made it that far, but you have had my heart and my body at your feet for six months, you faithless little termagant."

"I'm not…"

"You are. You take everything I do and say and interpret it with the worse possible connotations. You do not trust me. You even reject my declaration of love. You have no faith in me at all!"

"I…" She couldn't think of what to say in her own defense, which was an awful admission that she didn't have one.

He glared down at her. "I thought I could not get a woman pregnant. You cannot know what that did to me, but I believed I had nothing to offer a relationship of longevity."

"Babies aren't the only thing that matters in marriage."

"That is easy for you to say. You don't know the pain of wanting and never having. Bianca knew and it tore her apart." He stopped speaking and swallowed as if the pain was too much for him to bear. "She killed herself rather than face a future without children. I was not enough for her. I could not give her what she wanted most."

"No…if she'd killed herself…" It would have been

all over the press. "You're wrong. You blame yourself, but—"

"She did a pregnancy test that morning. It was negative…they were all negative." He took a deep breath, his big body taut with pain. "She went walking along the cliffs."

"And the ground gave way beneath her. That isn't suicide, Marcello."

"She could have thrown herself to safety…if she had wanted to."

Horror gripped Danette's heart. "You don't really believe that. It's not true."

"You were not there."

"Neither were you. She fell, Marcello. She didn't jump. She wouldn't have jumped. She had too much to live for."

"What had she to live for? Her dreams were in ashes in the waste bin of our en suite. One more pregnancy test. One more disappointment."

"If she wanted to be a mother that badly, she would have tried in vitro, or adoption."

"She said we were young, that we had time."

"And she meant it."

"You did not hear her crying at night when she thought I was asleep."

"I'm sorry if this hurts you, but those tears were probably for you. She knew how proud you are, how much not being able to make her pregnant hurt you. She loved you, of course she cried. She shed the tears you would not shed for yourself." She groped for corroboration. "If she'd been as deeply unhappy as you think she was, don't you think the press would have picked up on it? They would have had a field day with that kind of grief."

"They printed plenty of pictures of her looking un-happy."

"And you believed the pictures?"

"They do not lie."

"The camera lies all the time. If you get a picture of me first waking up in the morning, I look unhappy. I don't wake up for at least an hour and two cups of coffee. You scowl when you read the stock reports, but that doesn't mean you are unhappy."

"You don't know what it was like."

"No. But I can guess. Bianca loved you, like I love you. It hurt her to see you hurting."

He snorted at that. "You cannot say you share that affliction."

"Oh, yes, I can. I would have walked away from you rather than trap you in a relationship you didn't want. I finally agreed to marry you when I understood it would hurt you more for me to say no than to live in a marriage thrust on you by my pregnancy."

"But you said—"

"Some face-saving stuff, some stuff that was true, but wasn't the whole picture. Marcello, you aren't at fault for Bianca's death."

The ferocious tension in him arced higher rather than depleting. "Maybe you are right."

And she understood the increased tension. Marcello needed a catharsis for his pain, but he would not let himself cry. He was too strong, too macho for that outlet.

She brought his face down to hers and pressed her open mouth to his, taking the kiss to a level of hungry desire that could only be satisfied by two naked bodies writhing together on a bed. They made love in a firestorm of need and she screamed her love for him when she reached orgasm, only to have the words repeated fiercely back to her as he shattered.

He collapsed on top of her. "That was amazing."

"Yes, it was."

"You do not think we hurt the baby?"

"No, but he's probably going to be born with a love for storms after that."

Marcello laughed softly, but then he met her gaze, his own so serious, she ached for him. "I've carried that burden of guilt for four years."

"But it was a false burden."

"She was too young to die. I thought it had to be someone's fault."

"And you were already busy feeling like you'd let her down in the marriage stakes. It was easy to take the blame."

"Yes."

"But it wasn't your fault and you didn't let her down. Marcello, she was still young. She was probably glad in some ways she hadn't conceived yet."

He carefully disengaged and rolled off of Danette and then propped himself on his elbow at her side and laid his other hand possessively over her womb. "She refused to try in vitro."

"Maybe she felt guilty about that, too."

"Maybe."

"Do you feel better?"

"When I am with you, I always feel better."

"I'm glad."

"There was a lot of miscommunication in my marriage with Bianca, or maybe lack of communication is the better term, and it hurt us both. I don't want that with you."

"I don't, either."

"I refused to believe you loved me when you told me the first few times."

"I remember. Are you saying you believe me now?"

"Yes. I have to. You were willing to marry me believing I still loved a dead woman."

"It's okay that you still love her."

"But that love is in my past. You refuse to believe my vow of love today."

"I—"

"I do love you, more than life itself. I am sorry I was so messed up about marriage, but I want our marriage to be based on honesty and true understanding."

"Yes…"

He nodded, took a deep breath and then said, "I want to wait to get married until I have convinced you of the reality of my feelings."

"What?" She couldn't believe what she was hearing. "What if that took a long time? What if I didn't believe you until after the baby was born? This is crazy."

"Then so be it. I will marry you, Danette, make no mistake, but I will not build the foundations of the rest of our lives on mistrust."

His words went through her heart like a blazing sword. He had to love her to be willing to risk the illegitimacy of his child. He was telling her in an unmistakable way that there was nothing more important in life than she was to him.

Her eyes filled with tears as a glorious smile spread across her face. "I do believe you. I do."

He gave her a narrow-eyed look. "You are sure?"

"I've never been so sure of anything."

He breathed in a sigh of relief as if the weight of the

world had finally been lifted from his shoulders. "*Te amo, amante*. I love you with all my heart."

"And I love you."

They made love again, this time finishing the tender beginning they had had when they first came into the room. He took a long time arousing her and reveled in every touch she directed at him. When he penetrated her softness, he set a slow, love-filled rhythm that brought them to a mutual climax that shattered them both.

Tomasso and Maggie's wedding went off without a hitch and Danette finally got to meet the other sister-in-law, Therese. She'd been staying with Maggie, helping her with the wedding preparations.

Danette stood beside Marcello while Tomasso and Maggie spoke their vows under the pavilion on their private beach. It was a beautiful ceremony and Danette found herself wiping her eyes several times as the couple spoke their vows with obvious love and devotion.

Marcello's arm came around her and he whispered in her ear. "Soon, that will be us, *amante mia*."

She nodded, swallowing back more tears of poignant emotion.

He kissed her temple. "I love you."

She turned her head and kissed his shoulder, giving him her love silently.

Afterward, the family teased her about being emotional because she was pregnant, but Therese smiled and laid a gentle hand on her arm. "I think it is very sweet."

She smiled back at the sister-in-law she knew she would love despite the fact she barely knew her and the other woman's background was so different than her own. Therese Scorsolini was far too kind and friendly to intimidate Danette.

"It's just so neat to see Tomasso and Maggie so happy together. It's the way marriage should be, you know?"

Therese's beautiful brown eyes filled with a sadness that Danette did not understand. "Yes, that is how it should be," was all she said, however.

Flavia sighed and the look she gave King Vincente accused without giving a clue as to what she was holding him accountable for.

"What?" he asked, sounding bewildered and very much like a man and not a king.

Flavia shook her head. "I can see I should have taken things into hand years ago, but pride is a hard barrier to overcome."

After that incomprehensible speech, she asked Tomasso's children if they wanted to go for a walk on the beach. Upon receiving enthusiastic agreement, all three removed their shoes, left them under the pavilion and headed toward the waterline.

She stopped just as she was leaving the pavilion and turned her head back to catch King Vincente's eye. "Are you coming?"

"I am invited?" he asked, sounding as stunned as his three sons looked by the comment.

"But of course. Didn't I just say so?"

The king went, his expression one of a man totally bewildered by life.

Danette couldn't help laughing. "I wonder if she's decided to take a personal interest in him not growing into a lonely old man."

"You cannot be serious. For years, she wouldn't even allow his name to be spoken."

"Well, she's speaking it now, isn't she?" Danette asked and then added, "She loved him once."

"She stopped loving him years ago," Claudio, Marcello's oldest brother, said.

"True love does not die that easily," Therese said with an edge in her voice.

Marcello agreed. "No, it doesn't." He looked down at Danette, his eyes filled with fierce emotion. "I will love you forever."

She stared at him, her heart squeezing so tight, she could barely breathe. "And I will always love you."

He kissed her, and the sound of his brothers' laughter faded as the man she knew would be part of her heart for eternity showed her she would also be part of his.